John Kevin comes to Ireland every summer with his mother, and leaves London behind him for the sunshine and countryside of Ireland, the company of his six cousins, and the life of Ballydawn.

Running through all these summers is his friendship with his cousin Mattie, and their gradual understanding as the Troubles worsen that the world can be a much darker place than Ballydawn lets on.

John O'Donoghue is the author of *Brunch Poems* (Waterloo Press, 2009); *Fools & Mad* (Waterloo Press, 2014); and *Sectioned: A Life Interrupted* (John Murray, 2009). *Sectioned* was awarded Mind Book of The Year 2010. His story 'The Irish Short Story That Never Ends' won The Irish Post Creative Writing Competition in 2016. He was awarded a Brookleaze Grant by the Royal Society of Literature, also in 2016, to work on a novel about John Clare and Robert Lowell, both patients in the same asylum over 100 years apart. He is a Lecturer in Creative Writing at the University of Brighton.

A magical experience. By turns sad, funny, dark and lovely, John O'Donoghue introduces us to a rich set of characters in the long summer days of what seems a distant, warmer time.

Mick Finlay, author of the *Arrowood* novels

"We're flesh and blood, John Kevin. Cousins. You're a part of me, and I'm a part of you."
What if the past is another country that is nearly but not quite yours? John O'Donoghue's short stories explore the emigrant experience through the often minute details that differentiate neighbouring cultures. John Kevin is an innocent abroad not in a foreign country, but in the country of his parents' birth. He must navigate the familiar and unfamiliar with only his own inherited instincts to guide him.

Nessa O'Mahony, writer

These stories from childhood summers in Ireland are written with delicacy and tact, their solid realism mingled with the magic of childish imagination

Tessa Hadley, writer

Also by John O'Donoghue
Sectioned: A Life Interrupted (John Murray, 2009)
Brunch Poems (Waterloo Press, 2009)
Fools & Mad (Waterloo Press, 2014)

Some of these stories were first published in
*Aesthetica, The Frogmore Papers, The Irish Times, The
London Magazine* and *The Stinging Fly*.

In memory of my mother and father, my aunt and
uncle, my cousin Johnny, and his son Kevin.
'Like dolmens round my childhood, the old people.'

The King From Over the Water

John O'Donoghue

the wild
geese
press

First published in 2019 by
The Wild Geese Press

the wild
geese
press

A CIP record for this book is available from The British Library

ISBN 978-1-9993753-0-0

Printed in Great Britain by Lightning Source UK Ltd

Ballydawn doesn't exist. But it did, once upon a time. The author of this book is happy that Ballydawn can be shared in its pages with others who may have been there, and those coming for the first time.

Contents

PART I:
THE YOUNG PRETENDER

A Crossing

The wind blows great gusts off the sea and the stars twinkle. The big boat stands waiting.

We walk up the gangplank where a short sailor, gnarly and grey, holds out a hand. The boat throbs. I throb too: it is exciting to be going on the big boat.

I look back to the hills. The town's fairylights glitter in the darkness. It seems as if the night is absorbing them all. The sailor takes my hand and helps me up. He smiles and my mother smiles too.

"Has he got sealegs?"

"Sure hasn't he one marked port and the other starboard!"

The sailor laughs.

Starboard. What is that? Is that where you see the stars?

"Come on John," says my mother. "We must find a seat."

We walk to the very top of the gangplank and through to a big lounge. The lights are bright and I blink. There are lots of people. Cases and bags lie everywhere. The seats are in rows, like armchairs, but all stuck together. They are yellow and the lights are yellow too. The boat throbs. I can feel it in my tummy.

My mother finds two seats for us at the far end of the lounge under a small round window. She puts her big black bag in front of her seat and we sit down.

"Now," she says. "We'll soon be there."

"What is starboard?" I ask. "Is it where you can see the stars?

Can I go there?"

"Starboard? That's what sailors mean when they say right. Port is on the left and starboard in on the right."

"Why do they have different words?"

"Because they have a special sailors' language. They call the boat 'she'. To them the boat is a lady."

How could the boat be a lady?

A young woman comes and stands in front of the seat next to my mother's.

"Is anyone sitting here?"

"No," says my mother.

"Do you mind if I take it?"

"Not at all," says my mother.

The young woman sits down.

"Is this your son?" she asks. "How old are you, little fella?"

"Five and a half," I say.

"Aren't you a big boy for five and a half?"

I blush and say nothing.

"He's shy," says my mother.

The young woman is very pretty. She is blonde with nice eyes and wears a suede jacket and jeans. My mother never wears jeans.

"Where are you going?" she asks my mother.

"We're going to Ballydawn," says my mother. "In Monaghan. Do you know it around there?"

"I think I've heard of it," says the young woman. "I'm from Dublin myself. Are you going over for a holiday?"

"We are," says my mother.

"That's nice," says the pretty young woman.

"My name's Mary," says my mother, "and this is John Kevin."

"How do you do?" says the pretty young woman. "I'm Anna. I work in Guy's Hospital. All bedpans and backache. And the odd hooley! You wouldn't watch my bag till I get a breath of fresh air out the deck? I won't be too long."

"Of course," says my mother.

When Anna is gone my mother says, "Don't say a word about why we're going over, do you hear?"

I look at my mother.

"Do you hear?" she says. I nod.

"That's a good boy," she says.

"Are we ever going back?" I ask.

"We'll see," she says, "we'll see."

The boat gives a big loud throb and I can feel it move. Now we are sailing out to sea. The waves are flowing beneath us. The stars are out on the starboard side and the port is behind on the port side. It is exciting, but I'm not excited any more. I curl up on the seat and try to sleep.

But it is too bright and yellow to sleep and there is too much noise. I can hear men singing and wonder if it is the sailors singing their sea shanties. The boat rolls and throbs and it makes my tummy dizzy. Anna comes back.

"And where's your husband?" she asks my mother.

"He gets sick on the boat," my mother says. "So he stays home and paints the house."

I think of home. Why does my mother call it a house? We live in a small flat, in an attic.

"I'm sure he'll be missing you. Are you going for long?"

"Just a while," says my mother. "Come on, John," she says, "I'd better take you for a wee wee. Would you watch that bag of mine, Anna?"

"Of course, Mary," says Anna. My mother takes me out on deck.

"She's the nosey one, isn't she? 'And where's your husband?' Say nothing to her, do you hear me?" I nod and yawn.

The wind is cold now, and fresh, and darkness has deepened all around. The waves lap at the boat as it ploughs through the deep black sea. I can't see any stars from this side of the boat, nor the moon either. I look at my mother and think of my father's eyes, of him asking me to stay, of the look in them as I went to her.

"We'll soon be there," says my mother, and I hold her hand as we go back inside. The singing is louder now and I wish I knew the words.

The Unicorn

Well, John, would you know your Auntie Annie?"
We get out of my uncle's car and there is my aunt. She is like my mother, only taller. I say nothing.

"Come in," says my aunt. "I have the kettle on."

A gaggle of hens follows her as she goes towards the house. It is a big house, with grey walls and a black roof. We follow behind my aunt and the hens and when we get to the door of the house she shoos the hens away.

"I see you still have the horse," says my uncle. We all stop at the door. My uncle is looking across to a field where a big white horse is eating the grass. He is the biggest creature I have ever seen, like a horse a knight would have.

"That oul' beast?" says my aunt. "Sure he's about ready for the knacker's yard. But I think we'll get another year or two out of him yet."

"What do you call him?" says Mattie. Mattie is my cousin. He is my age, or a bit older. He's bigger than me, but I think I will catch him up.

"We call him Neddy," says my aunt. "Would you like to get up on him? Are you a bit of a cowboy, Mattie?"

My mother and my uncle smile, but Mattie isn't smiling.

"Of course I'm a cowboy," says Mattie. "I'm the fastest draw in the West."

The grown-ups laugh.

We go into the house and have tea and cake and biscuits and the grown-ups talk about the farm and how everyone is and how long we'll be over for. Mattie and I play cowboys until we are put out in the yard.

"Phew! Phew!"

Mattie fires his gun at me. I take cover by a wheelbarrow and shoot back.

"Phew! Phew!"

Mattie rolls over, holding his tummy.

I run across to him.

"It's no use," he says, lying on his back looking up at me. "I'm a goner. Bury me with my guns. And say on my tombstone I was the fastest draw in the West. Until I met the Cockney Kid."

He means me. But what is a Cockney?.

He shuts his eyes and dies with a long groan.

"I'll be back tomorrow," says my uncle.

The grown-ups have finished their tea and are all talked out. We are staying the night in my aunt's farmhouse. I have never been to a farm before, or stayed in a farmhouse.

My mother and my aunt all stand at the door as my uncle walks to his car. Mattie and I are sitting on two buckets we've turned the wrong way up. We are cowboys. I am the Cockney Kid and he is Mattie Two-Guns Murphy. We squint at my uncle as he comes towards us. Partly because of the sunlight. Partly because we are cowboys.

"I'll see you lads tomorrow," says my uncle. "Make sure you're good boys and do all you're told."

"Goodbye, Daddy," says Mattie, and my uncle winks at us, gets into his car and drives off.

"Ride 'em, cowboy!"

Mattie is up on the big white horse.

"Gee up, Neddy!" he says.

Neddy stands still and looks ahead, as if he's heard something. My aunt has a hold of his bridle, but there's no saddle. Mattie is riding the horse bareback. But, as Neddy is standing still, I wonder if Mattie is really riding him? Surely he should be moving if he was riding Neddy?

It is very warm now. The hens are clucking in the yard and my mother is feeding them, throwing some kind of light brown seeds on the ground they all rush to peck at. Some of the hens peck at each other.

The hills around the farm are covered in sunlight. The air is fresh. In the trees at the end of the field birds are singing.

"Attaboy!"

Neddy looks like the unicorn in the story I read on the boat. But he's bigger and doesn't have a horn. Or at least, he isn't showing his horn. Perhaps he's got a horn which he hides when people are around. Perhaps it twists back into his head. Otherwise people would know he was a unicorn and would want to catch him. It said in my story that Noah brought all the animals into the Ark, but the unicorns were playing in the forest and wouldn't come when he called. I asked my mother if there really were unicorns. She said I'd be asking her next if there were leprechauns.

"Do you want to get up on Neddy yourself, John?" says my aunt.

Neddy looks round. Does he know what my aunt is saying? There is something scary about Neddy.

I run crying from the field into my mother's arms.

I can hear his hooves behind me. He is snorting and panting, and his hooves are coming closer every second. I run and run but he is catching me up. Ahead is the boat, big against the quay. The gangplank is down and an old bearded man stands at the top of it. He is calling me to him, me and whatever is behind me.

I look around over my shoulder. It is Neddy, Neddy with his horn out. He really is a unicorn!

But the gangplank is being raised and the old bearded man is going inside the big boat. I know now that he is Noah and that Neddy and me have been shut out of the Ark.

Rain starts to fall, big fat drops of rain, and Neddy rears up. His hooves are in the air, and he is about to trample me. The rain falls in a huge downpour and suddenly I am soaked.

"John! John! Wake up! It's all right, it's only a dream!"

I am in a strange bed. My mother is leaning over me, and in the moonlight I can make out her shadowy figure. Mattie is lying beside me, and now he starts to stir.

But it's as if the dream hasn't ended at all. For I am soaked. The sheets are soaked. Mattie and my mother are soaked.

I have wet the bed.

My uncle's car pulls into the yard.

"Well!" he shouts from the rolled down window. "Are you ready? Did you have a nice time? Did anyone get up on the horse?"

My mother says goodbye to my aunt. She tells her that she is sorry, but my aunt says not to worry, it's just one of those things.

We walk towards my uncle's car. Mattie runs ahead and opens the door.

"John Kevin wet the bed, Daddy!"

I blush but say nothing. I look across to the field where Neddy is chomping at the grass. He lifts his head to look at me. I know he knows. About him being a unicorn. Sure enough there is a grey star on his head. This must be where the horn twists out when he is haunting your dreams. He looks away and goes back to chomping the grass.

My mother pulls my hand.

"Come on," she says. "I haven't all day."

I walk with her to the car. We get in and my uncle turns the key that makes the car start. As the engine roars I hear Neddy neighing in the field. We pull away and Mattie laughs and soon the farm is far behind us.

Kissing Cousins

The front garden is lush and green. Each blade of grass is vivid in the warm golden sunshine and the big hedges enclose us to make a box of velvet. Behind us, the bungalow's stippled walls are white and I think of green, white and gold, of the flag and shamrocks and the harp. This is Ireland and we are home for the summer.

Mary has the ball. She stands with her back to us and tosses it over her head.

"Queenie-i-o, who's got the ball?

Is he large or is he small?

Is she short or is she tall?

Queenie-i-o, who's got the ball?"

It lands in front of me and I run forward to scoop it up. I rush back and get into line just in time. Mary has turned round and is looking hard at each of us.

Geraldine, Mattie, Evelyn, Anna and me. All in line. All with our hands behind our backs. Only I have the ball. But it could be any one of us.

"It might be Anna," says Mary, "or it could be you, Geraldine."

Not until Mary accuses one of us directly do we have to tell her. If she is wrong, though, she must do it all again. Mary is trying to make us laugh. We might drop the ball if we laugh. It is important to keep a straight face.

"John Kevin, do you have the ball?"

How did she guess? But I am giving nothing away.

"You childer! Your dinner is ready!"

9

Auntie Lizzie calls us from the front door. Geraldine, Mattie, Evelyn and Anna all rush off for their dinner. Only Mary and I are left.

"So, John Kevin," she says. "Do you have the ball or don't you?"

"Give me a kiss and I'll tell you."

"John Kevin!" she cries. "Don't be so bold!"

"Just a little one," I say.

She walks towards me, smiling, and kisses my lips. I close my eyes. Her lips are soft and I like to kiss her. I drop the ball. As I do, she bites my lip.

"Now!" she says. "That'll teach you to be so bold!"

And she runs off to her dinner.

I touch my lip. It is not too sore. But why did Mary bite me? I go in for my dinner. I hope it is not ham and potatoes. We had ham and potatoes yesterday.

"You be the Daddy and I'll be the Mammy."

Anna's dolly has no arms or hair and one eye seems to be turned back in its head. The dolly has no clothes either, not even a nappy. It must be a girl dolly because it has no willy.

"OK, Anna," I say.

"Now, Dolly," says Anna. "You be a good girlie till your Daddy gets home, otherwise he might scold you. "

My Daddy never scolds me. And I wouldn't scold Dolly. She looks like she has suffered enough already.

"What's that, Dolly? If you're good will Daddy bring you sweeties? He surely will, pet, won't you John Kevin?"

We are by the river at the bottom of the back garden, although it is more of a back field than a back garden. Uncle Tommy grows vegetables in it and has planted trees at the front of the field, near the bungalow. They are apple trees and Auntie Lizzie makes them into apple pies and apple sauce for the roast pork on Sundays. Auntie Lizzie is always cooking, bread, scones, cakes. And lovely Sunday roasts with apple sauce and delicious apple pies. But I think Auntie Lizzie is too fond of ham. And potatoes.

"I'll give Dolly an apple from the tree," I say.

"Oh, isn't that a lovely Daddy, Dolly? Come here Daddy till the

Mammy gives you a kiss."

Anna is very pretty. But I am scared she might bite me. She leans towards me and we kiss. I like Anna. She doesn't bite.

"Now you childer. I've only Aggie and Gusty to do and then we're done."

I am in Uncle Tommy's post van. Uncle Tommy delivers newspapers and parcels to farms on his route. He loves driving the van and taking us with him. It is fun being driven in the post van with Uncle Tommy. It roars and rumbles up hill and down dale. I do not know what a dale is but I think it must be the opposite of a hill. We have been learning about opposites with Miss Farrell. Miss Farrell says that opposites attract. I am not sure what this means but it sounds very clever.

"Did you know," I say to Anna, "opposites attract?"

"Attract what, John Kevin?"

"I don't know," I say. "Other opposites?"

"Opposites attract each other," says Mary. Mary is a year older than us and she is very clever. She knows all of her tables. I only the one, two and three times tables. But I am learning.

"We're here," says Uncle Tommy. "You childer can sit in the back of the van. I'll open the doors. Let the air at you."

He stops the van. A man and a woman appear at the end of the lane. Uncle Tommy opens the door and gets out. He says hello to the man and the woman and then he opens the door for us. Mary, Anna and I all get down. It is very high up in the van and Uncle Tommy helps us. He is smiling and I know he is in a good mood. He has been to Jimmy's Bar. Whenever he goes to Jimmy's Bar he always comes out of it in a good mood. My mother says it is because of something called whiskey. You can only buy whiskey in bars. It is like a special medicine they sell there.

Mary, Anna and I walk around to the back of the van with Uncle Tommy. He opens the back doors for us with his key and we sit on the cold metal. Anna and I hold hands and soon we are kissing. I like kissing Anna more than Mary because Anna doesn't bite.

I am just about to ask Mary if she wants a kiss. Even though she bites when she kisses I do not want her to feel left out. But she runs off and I do not know what to do.

Uncle Tommy appears in front of the van doors.

"You two! Stop that! That's very dirty what you're doing!"

"Yes, Daddy," says Anna. "We're very sorry, Daddy."

Mary is looking at us. She is smiling and I can see that she has told Uncle Tommy about Anna and I kissing each other.

Uncle Tommy is not in a good mood now. He says goodbye to the man and the lady and we drive off back to Ballydawn. I want to hold Anna's hand but feel I shouldn't. I am very sad. Anna is sad too. But I do not think Mary is sad at all. I do not understand girls.

Or grown-ups.

Or kissing.

The Bogey Man

It is very hot. I am walking down the road with my cousins. We pass by white houses with big front gardens behind big green hedges. The houses lie back from the road and they all look like my aunt and uncle's house. The houses are bungalows. It means the houses have no upstairs – all of the rooms are downstairs.

They are very modern.

Like televisions

"Keep in!" shouts Mattie.

Everyone steps to the side of the road. There is a gap and I fall into it. A car comes towards us and roars past, smoke coming out of the back.

"Are you all right, John Kevin?" says Geraldine.

Geraldine is the eldest of the girls. She has a kind face and eyes like my mother's. She is bending down to look at me. I try not to cry. My ankle hurts where it twisted.

"He'll live," says Johnny. "The ditch isn't going to kill this bucko."

Johnny is the eldest. He has black hair and the same blue eyes as Geraldine only a bit darker. My mother is always saying he looks like Elvis. I think Elvis may be one of the neighbours. Johnny bends down and grips my hand. He pulls me up and I come out of the ditch.

"Now," says Johnny. "Will you be able to get as far as Ballydawn? Or do you want us to take you home?"

"I'm OK," I say.

"Come on," says Mattie.

My cousins turn towards Ballydawn. Johnny and Geraldine are at the front and the rest of us are behind them – Mattie and me, then Mary and Evelyn and Anna.

"Will we call in on Frank Donegan?" says Anna. She is at the back with Mary and Evelyn so she has to shout to be heard.

"We will," says Geraldine. "But don't be making a show of yourself."

"How would I be making a show of myself?" says Anna.

"Just be a good girl and wait your turn," says Geraldine.

We all come to a stop.

Johnny and Geraldine cross the road and signal for the rest of us to come. A big white building with a red tin roof stands behind them. We all cross the road in single file. As we get near I can hear a terrible noise, clanging and sloshing and splashing.

"Were you ever in a creamery?" says Mattie.

I shake my head.

We go into the white building. The floor is all ridged and clear water and grey water runs down the ridges. There is lots of machinery and men in overalls walking around hauling big metal cans across the floor.

It is very noisy.

"Frank Donegan works here, John Kevin!" Johnny shouts at me. "That's him over there. Come on to he gets a look at you."

Frank Donegan is standing by some kind of machine.

He smiles when he sees us.

"Is this Mary Murphy's boy?" he says.

"This is John Kevin," says Johnny. "All the way from London, England. Will you put him up on the scales, Frank?"

"Come on, John Kevin," says Frank Donegan. "We'll soon see if you're a heavyweight, a featherweight, or just a tiny wee paperweight."

I step up onto his machine. He starts fiddling with the metal bar across the top, sliding bits up and down it until the bar sits level.

"There," he says. "Three stone exactly. You're so light it's a wonder you don't blow away."

I go red and step off the machine.

He weighs the rest of my cousins. Only Mary and Evelyn and Anna are lighter than me. But he doesn't say any of them will blow away.

Johnny thanks him and Frank Donegan takes a bag of bulls' eyes out of his overalls and give us all one. We come out into the sunshine. We cross the road and walk over the bridge and into the village. I am careful crossing the bridge in case the wind blows me away and into the river.

It is only when I get to the village that I feel safe.

We are past the creamery on the road home. We have eaten our ice creams and are walking in silence. It is still very hot. We reach the bungalows. A man is looking at me through his window. I can see him over the hedge. He has a big black beard and is scowling. Suddenly he raises his fist and shakes it at me.

I run forward to be with Johnny and Geraldine. I am crying. The man with the beard is very scary. I am afraid he will come out of his bungalow and chase me.

"What's the matter, John Kevin?" says Johnny.

Mattie catches up.

"It's the Bogey Man!" says Mattie. "John Kevin looked at him! Now he's going to come and eat us all! Run!"

Johnny and Geraldine stop for a moment and look at each other.

"Run for it!" they shout. "The Bogey Man is coming!"

We all run. I do not look behind me. But I am sure I can hear the Bogey Man, running and stumbling, huffing and puffing, grumbling and growling. He is the Giant and I am Jack at the top of the beanstalk. He can smell the blood of an Englishman. He will eat me if he catches me. I'm falling behind. My cousins are in front of me – they are nearly at my aunt and uncle's house. The air is rushing past my ears as I run. But it is no good. One by one my cousins disappear through the gate and round the corner of the gravel driveway. I can hear the Bogey Man now. I can feel his breath on my neck. I look behind me. I turn and step on something. My sore ankle twists and I fall over.

The Bogey Man will surely catch me now. He is going to take me home and put me in his pot. He is going to eat me.

"John!"

It is my mother.

"What are you doing down there?"

I look around.

The Bogey Man has disappeared.

She runs over and picks me up. She carries me into my aunt and uncle's house. My cousins are all grinning in the kitchen. She takes me into our bedroom and lays me down on the bed.

"What's the matter?" she says.

I tell her about the Bogey Man.

She starts to laugh.

"That's no Bogey Man!" she says. "That's Mickey McDevitt. He was over in London at the start of the War and joined up. He was never the same when he came back. Shell shock. Now let's have a look at you."

It is the evening. My cousins are playing outside in the front garden and I am lying on my bed.

My ankle has swollen and I have to rest it. I am thinking about what my mother said. About the Bogey Man and shell shock.

Why would anyone be shocked by shells?

Perhaps when he was in the War he was captured by Mermen, who took him to the King of the Mermen's Palace. Perhaps he was put in a cage and the Young Princes teased him. Perhaps they had shells they shook at him. And then when he escaped and came back home whenever he saw shells they upset him. And this is why he wants to eat children.

That must be it.

I go back to reading my copy of *The Dandy*.

It will not be long to dinner time.

"How's that ankle, John Kevin?"

It is very hot, hotter than last time. I am walking down the road with my cousins. We pass by the white bungalows with big front gardens behind big green hedges. We are going to Ballydawn to get messages.

Messages are errands.

They are not real messages.

I look at Johnny. He is standing at the side of the road where the ditch is. I won't be falling into the ditch this time. Now I know about ditches I will be OK.

"My ankle is fine, thank you, Johnny."

"Come on, slow coach! There's ice creams waiting for us at JonJo's. They'll all be melted if we don't get a move on."

Johnny turns and leads us down the road.

There are no cars today and the sky is very blue. There are no clouds either just the big yellow sun. I think about ice cream and wonder if the creamery makes ice cream. We are just coming up to the creamery. We come near the last of the bungalows, where the Bogey Man lives. I wonder if he is in today. I turn around to look.

I can see him in his window. But he is not scowling today. Or shaking his fist.

He is crying, holding his head in his hands, crying like a big baby.

I am puzzled at first. Then I remember the shells. I think it must be because of them, because of the King of the Mermen and his Palace and being a held in a cage and the Young Princes teasing him by shaking shells at him. But I wonder where he has seen them. There are no shells in Ballydawn. I stop and stare. For some reason he looks up. Tears are streaming down his face and into his beard. His face is twisted. I feel very sorry for the poor Bogey Man.

"Come on!" barks Johnny.

I turn slowly and follow him down the road. I do not want to keep Johnny waiting. We have messages to get. And besides, the ice creams in JonJo's are the nicest ice creams there are.

A Visit from Grandpa

We are going next door to the McEntees. They have a television and we are going to watch the news.

"Come on!" says Uncle Tommy. "We'll be late!"

He is standing by the door to the kitchen ready to go. We are all behind him, Auntie Lizzie, my six cousins, my mother, and me. Uncle Tommy has changed into his suit, the one he wears for Mass, and has his hat on. Auntie Lizzie has taken off her apron and is wearing her flyaway specs and her Sunday dress, and my mother is wearing her best dress too.

"Mattie!" says Auntie Lizzie. "You can't go to the McEntees with a face like that! Come here to I give you a scrub!"

She grabs Mattie and pulls him to her. A hankie is in her hand and she puts the tip of it to her red lips. She licks the tip and starts rubbing at Mattie's face. He squirms but she dabs away at him.

"Mammy! Would you quit!" cries Mattie.

"Come on!" roars Uncle Tommy. "We'll be late for him!"

We all go through the kitchen and out the back door. It is a sunny day, warm and golden. The light on the big hedge between us and the McEntees flows down the green leaves like bubbles of amber. It is good to be in Ireland on a day like this.

"Where's Grandpa?" asks Johnny. "Is Grandpa not coming to see the news?"

"He said he'd meet us at the gate at five to six," says Uncle Tommy. He looks at his watch. "It's ten to now."

We come to the gate. Uncle Tommy stops and looks down the road. I look down the road too. A tall thin man in a shirt with no collar, black trousers and big boots is walking towards us. He is carrying something in his hand.

"Well," says Uncle Tommy as the man gets closer. "I see you brought your fiddle, Daddy."

"Well," says the man. "Every king deserves a minstrel."

"This is your grandfather," says my mother. "Say hello, John."

I am too shy to say hello. I hide behind my mother and take a peep at my grandfather. He must be very old. He has white hair.

"Come on," says Uncle Tommy. "We don't want to miss it."

We all follow him to the McEntees' gate. Uncle Tommy opens the gate and we walk down behind him to the McEntees' front door. Just as we get there the door opens.

"Hello, Tommy," says Mrs McEntee. She is wearing a black dress with pearls around her neck.

"Well, Rita," says Uncle Tommy. "You look like you're off to Hollywood for your Oscar."

Mrs McEntee laughs, and says hello to the rest of us, and shows us in to her living room. Mr McEntee is sitting on a big white sofa. Beside him are his son, Paul, and his daughter, Marie. The McEntees have brought in chairs from the kitchen and we all sit down to watch the television.

I look around the room. There is a fireplace with plastic logs and a red light behind them. The fireplace is set back into a little wall of light brown bricks all different sizes and there is a statue of the Infant of Prague in the middle of the mantelpiece. On the wall above is a picture of Our Lord, with his Sacred Heart exposed. My aunt and uncle have the same picture but I notice that the McEntees have a gold frame.

"How's business?" asks Uncle Tommy.

"Ah, the best," says Mr McEntee. "Post Office treating you well, Tommy?"

"Well enough," says Uncle Tommy.

"I see you've brought your fiddle," says Mr McEntee to my grandfather. "Will you be giving us a tune?"

"I might give you a few," says my grandfather. "If you have plenty of stout."

Mr McEntee grins.

"I got in some specially," he says. He turns to his son, who is about my cousin Johnny's age, seven or perhaps eight. "Paul," he says, "put on that television! He should be coming on now."

Paul gets up and turns on the television. The screen flickers and the set hums and then it is on.

A man wearing a dark suit with a white shirt and a dark tie is talking to a big crowd. He has a round face and hair like a loaf of bread that's just risen. He looks familiar but I cannot think where I have seen him before.

"If the day was clear enough and you went down to the bay and looked west and your sight was good enough you could see Boston, Massachusetts. And if you did you would see down working on the docks there Dohertys, Flahertys, Ryans, and cousins of yours who had gone across to Boston and made good."

He stops and smiles, his white teeth bright in the black and white of the TV screen.

"I wonder perhaps how many of you here have a relative in America you would admit to? Hold up your hand."

All the grown-ups start laughing. Then I remember where I have seen the man on the television. We have a plate hanging over the mantelpiece of our flat in London. He is on the plate along with his wife. He is the President of America, but I cannot remember his name.

The man speaks some more and I try to listen like the rest but it is difficult. I am sitting next to Mary and Mary keeps pinching me. But I know we will get shouted at if we make any noise or wriggle around. So I pinch her back and bite my tongue when she gives me an extra hard pinch. It's not fair. Girls aren't supposed to pinch.

But then the news is over and the grown-ups are all standing.

"Come on," says Mr McEntee. "Let's go outside and have a ceilidh."

We all go out of the house and down the gravel drive to the gate. Mr McEntee comes out behind us with a little table and Mrs

McEntee puts bottles of drink on it. Paul and Marie have brought glasses in a box and Mrs McEntee starts pouring stout for the grown-ups and lemonade for us. There are packets of crisps as well, Taytos. I have never seen Taytos before and the lemonade is red. I have never seen that before either. But it is all delicious and now we are having a party.

"Will you give us a tune?" says Mr McEntee to my grandfather.

He puts down his glass of stout and lifts up the fiddle. I notice that two of the fingers he uses to finger the strings are bent over, like a claw. But this does not stop him. He plays the fiddle as well as anyone, fast jigs that has everyone happy. My mother takes hold of me and starts to dance me around, and then Uncle Tommy is dancing with Auntie Lizzie and Mr McEntee is dancing with Mrs McEntee and my cousins are all dancing with each other.

There are no cars on the road. The evening is warm and sunny. We go on like this until the sun starts to sink, my grandfather playing the fiddle and drinking in between tunes, the grown-ups and the rest of us dancing and talking. The grown-ups all speak about the man on the television, how handsome he is, how he looks like Mickey O'Shea who owns O'Shea's Garage, how he is one of our own.

Gradually the dusk starts to come. My grandfather stops playing and takes a big drink of his stout, emptying his glass in one go. He wipes his mouth on the back of his hand and puts the glass down on the table.

"I am an old man and I have lived a long time," he says. "But this is a day I never thought I'd live to see. My own father told me of the Famine, how terrible it was, people dying all around him. And now one of our own is the leader of the western world. Wonders will never cease."

He looks back down the road, the shadows gathering now.

"Soon I shall be dead. Remember me, an old man who lived between Famine and Feast. Our day is coming!"

He turns round and starts to walk away, and we watch in silence as he strides down the road, his long shadow swaying behind him.

I look down at the table. All of the red lemonade bottles are empty and the packets of Taytos eaten. I wonder if the dancing is over. I look up at the sky. The moon is out now and I shiver.

"Come on," says my mother. "It's time you said your prayers and went to bed."

She takes my hand and we walk off towards my aunt and uncle's house.

"And don't forget to say a prayer for your Grandpa," she says.

I can't be sure but I think she is crying. I squeeze her hand and she squeezes mine back. Soon I am in my pyjamas and kneeling by my bed. I bless myself and say my prayers. My mother tucks me in and I think of my grandfather, of him disappearing into the dusky evening, his long shadow behind him.

I fall asleep and dream I hear a fiddle playing, laughter on a summer's evening, the President asking me to put my hand up.

PART II:
BONNIE PRINCE CHARLIE

Between the Lines

'll only be gone for one night," said my mother. "Now you be a good boy until I get back."

She got into Jim Ryan's Beetle and they drove off. She was going to Mullingar to see her cousins, the Hegartys, and I watched the car until it disappeared out of sight, past the creamery, over the bridge and away, down roads and past fields where the country blushed in the sunshine and the cloudless sky was a huge blue space where night might never return.

"She'll be back soon enough," said Mattie. "Let's go and play a bit of football up in Ballydawn. We'll see if Rory and Fergus want a game."

We walked down the road together, two boys in shorts and shirtsleeves, snakebelts around our waists, socks round our ankles. The Beetle was now way out of sight, as the pair of us neared Maggie's Bar, the midday sun as hot as it had been all summer.

"Hey boys! Hold on!"

We turned around. It was James Handley, coming out of Maggie's, his dark suit and tweed cap identical to his twin John's. You'd only know it was James by the little finger he was missing from his left hand. We waited by the side of the road for him to catch up with us.

"Well, James," said Mattie, as he drew alongside. "How's it going?"

"Ah sure, the same as ever," said James. "I was just in there delivering a new pair of shoes to Maggie's husband."

"And were you taking your payment in whiskey and beer?" asked Mattie.

"Divil the bit," said James. "John would be scolding me if I did."

The two brothers, James and John, lived in a small cottage together in Ballydawn. They were the local cobblers and had been for as long anyone could remember. When you went into their place, a dark shack of a cottage, you could hardly see in front of you for smoke. Between the turf fire and the brothers' fondness for the fags the parlour seemed to be fogbound. Fagbound, Uncle Tommy called it. I'd heard tales that visitors had called on them and never found their way out again, although this was just a bit of blarney, according to my mother. But I wasn't so sure.

There was something odd right enough about the pair of them. I never heard of any grown up brothers living together in England, and the fact that they were twins only added to their mystery for me. For besides the fog in their cottage, you'd hardly get a word out of them, besides a few "Aye, faith ayes," sighed more than said, a tender resignation in their soft voices, as Mattie gave them news of the village, and the Post Office where his father worked. It was as if they were lost in clouds of Capstan and the smoky haze from the fire.

"Do you see this boy's mother has run off and left him?" said Mattie.

I blushed but said nothing. He was exaggerating, but like all exaggerations there was truth in what he said and I was too put out to say anything.

"Is that so?" said James. He was used to Mattie trying to get a rise out of people, especially the likes of me. "And where has she gone?"

"To Mullingar, to see her cousins."

"The Hegartys?"

"Aye."

We came to the bridge and I could see the river trickling sluggishly in the heat to the right of me. Across to the left and beyond lay the fields we cut across to Queenslough, the scatter of cottages beside the tiny lake. My mother had taken me swimming there yesterday, the two of us alone in a basin of warm water no bigger than a large deep pond. She told me she'd come here all the time when she was my age, and smiled at me, as if I was a souvenir of those days instead of a boy who wanted to play football like Georgie Best and take a walk on the moon. And now she was gone.

"I knew your mother well when she was younger," said James Handley.

We came to Ballydawn and passed the new white bungalows, Jonjo's shop, and the red doors of O'Reilly's garage.

"Come on boys," he said. "I've something to show you."

Mattie and I looked at each other, but said nothing. We followed James into his smoky cottage. It was like walking from light into darkness.

"Well, boys."

From a distant corner of the murky room came the same identical voice, muffled and husky.

"Well, John," answered Mattie.

"Sit down, boys, sit down," said James. The earthen floor, I saw as my eyes grew used to the dim light, was bare apart from a few lasts and pairs of boots lying about the place. The fire was smouldering in the grate, the smell of turf blending with John's fags, a red point at the far side of the hearth the only sign that he was in the room at all. It was a little like being polar explorers, I thought. We were adrift in thick blizzards of snow as we made our final push to the top of the mountain, all contact with Base Camp lost. Only these two native guides could save us...

Mattie and I sat on the settle by the window, daylight at its dirty edge, smears and smuts keeping in the dark, the four of us deep in sepia.

James disappeared into the mist, his dark back gradually becoming invisible as he moved over towards his brother. We could hear a drawer opening, a hand searching around for something inside and then there he was, emerging ghostlike out of the smoke, holding a framed photograph. He came and stood in front of us, handing me the picture.

"Now," he said. "Would you know who that was?"

I looked at the photograph. It was stained brown, as if it had been tinted various shades of tan and russet by the turf fire. Two figures looked out at me, a man and a young plump woman, aged about eighteen, standing by a low wall, her in a white dress, head thrown back laughing and him darksuited with a tweed cap slouched to one side. As I looked more closely I recognised the pair of them. It was my mother, and a much younger version of James. With a start I realised that he couldn't possibly be as old as I'd taken him for.

"It's you and my mother," I said.

"So it is, so it is. We used to do a line, you know. During the Fifties. We went to the odd dance and the pictures. And Twenty-five – your mother was a great one for the cards."

"Aye, faith, she was," sighed John. His whispered words barely seemed to reach us.

"Get away!" said Mattie. "Auntie Mary and you?"

I could feel myself blushing, but I wasn't sure why.

"That's right," said James. "Isn't it John?"

"Aye, faith, you're right," said John. "Sure Mary was a fine girl. Aye, faith, as fine as you'd like."

I couldn't see him through the smoky haze but I had a feeling his eyes were turned inward as he spoke, looking back nearly half a lifetime to when my mother might have stood by the fire in the same room I was in now. I wondered if it was any clearer then, if the daylight came in, if James and John hadn't yet taken up the fags. I was glad no one could see my blushes.

"So what happened?" asked Mattie.

"She went over to England for the nursing."

"Aye, faith, the nursing," said John.

"We wrote to each other for a while but then I got a letter from her and that put an end to that. Wait," he said. "I think I have it still."

He disappeared back into the thick haze of the room, and again I could hear him raking around in the drawer. Then he stepped softly forward and handed me a letter, still in its envelope.

"Go on," he said. "Read it."

I carefully eased the piece of paper out into the dim light and laid the envelope on the settle beside me. I noticed that the stamp was brown, with a picture of a king on it. My mother must have sent this letter when the Queen's father was still alive. I suddenly felt I was reading something out of history. I cleared my throat and read the words out slowly and clearly.

Dear James

I hope you are well, as I am myself TG. The work here is quite hard but I am coping and there is always the odd bit of sport to take your mind off making beds and obeying Matron. She is like the worst nun you've ever met, but about twice as fat.

I don't think I can afford to get over this summer, as the price of everything here in London is very expensive. I spend most of the week rubbing two ha'pennines together to see if I can make a third out of them but conjuring is an art I'll leave to your brother. Is he still at the card tricks? Tell him I was asking after him.

I hope you won't miss me too much. I'll be thinking of you, especially when the hay comes in. That was a grand summer we had last year, and a grand harvest too. I don't think most Londoners have ever seen a bit of hay, apart from a few Cockneys, who go off to Kent hop-picking when the autumn comes.

I have a hop to pick myself now, as some of the girls are wanting to go to a place called the Galtymore, but I fancy the Gresham as it's a bit easier to get to. What do you do for a hooley yourself these days? Are you still going up to the Four Seasons? Anyone you have your eye on?

Write to me when you get a chance,

yours,

Mary xxx

I looked up at James. He was smiling at me, and I wondered what would have happened if my mother had married him instead of my father.

"A fine girl," said John, "aye, faith, aye."

"James, John," said Mattie. "We've got to be going. We've a few messages to get for Mammy. See you another time, boys, OK?"

He stood up and took the letter from me.

"Here, James. You'll be wanting this back."

He gave James the letter and I handed him the envelope.

"Tell your mother I was asking after her," said James.

I mumbled something and Mattie and I walked out into dazzling sunlight and sweet fresh air.

"Hey! Boys!" shouted Mattie. Rory and Fergus were kicking a ball against the door of O'Reilly's garage, a few yards up the road from the brothers' cottage, and Rory turned round to say hello to Mattie and me.

"Well, Mattie," he called. "Well, John Kevin."

Fergus kicked the ball towards us and Mattie ran onto it and hit it as hard as he could with his right. It smacked against the doors of the garage with a loud thwack! He picked up the rebound and chipped it over to Rory. Rory headed it on to me and I caught it on the volley and smacked it hard against the garage doors too.

"What a goal!" crowed Mattie. I watched as the ball bounced back out towards him. He scooped it up with his left and started playing keepsie-upsie, talking while he kicked the ball from foot to foot. I thought it was the coolest thing I'd ever seen.

"Hey boys, you won't believe what's just happened. We met James Handley on the road up to you there and didn't he invite us home for a bit of craic. Well, no sooner were we through the door than he's telling John Kevin here about how he used to court his Mammy. Hops, dinners, harvests, the whole thing. I think he still has a notion of her, what do you think boys?"

I counted fifty kicks, right foot to left foot and back again, before I rushed him. I pushed him over and we rolled around in the dirt, punching and kicking each other, before the wheels of a car screeched to a halt beside us. We both stopped and looked up to see who it was.

It was Jim Ryan's Beetle, and my mother was getting out of it.

"What are you two playing at?" she cried. "Get into that car the pair of you immediately!"

We stood up and brushed ourselves off. Rory and Fergus started to snigger but my mother soon put a stop to that.

"And if you two think it's funny to see these boys fighting, well I'll be down to tell your mother and father all about you standing there watching them. And then letting them go at each other instead of stepping in like good decent boys to break them up! Get away on home now before I change my mind!"

Rory and Fergus slunk off like kicked dogs and Mattie and I got into the back of the Beetle. We seethed in silence on the way home, the pair of us fuming, ready to thump the daylights out of each other if one of us so much as sneezed. The car pulled into the gravel drive at the side of the house and Jim Ryan rolled the car on down and parked in the back yard

"Get into the house, the pair of you," said my mother. She got out of the car and we went inside. There was no one around. Auntie Lizzie must have had them all out picking up sticks down Cllintock's Lane.

"Now," she said. "Why were you two fighting?"

We stood in front of the range, silent, sulking.

"Right," she said. "The pair of you will sort out your differences before I leave here. I forgot a little present I bought for my cousins. Lucky I did or you two would be cut and cullopped like a pair of little ruffians. Fighting in the road! Have you no shame? John, come with me and help me look for it."

I followed her into our room. She shut the door and hissed, "What the hell were you fighting about? What is wrong with you?"

I looked at her and bit my lip.

"Well?" she said.

"Mattie was teasing me," I said.

"What about?"

I hesitated.

"Well? Come on! I don't have all day!"

I told her what had happened, about meeting James Handley, about the letter, about Mattie telling Rory and Fergus the whole story.

My mother held me to her.

"Oh, John," she laughed. "Were you fighting for my honour?"

I pushed her away, my face hot now with tears.

"You're just teasing me as well!" I shouted.

"John, John! Would you hold on a minute? You have to read that letter between the lines. Sure, I'd met your father by the time I sent it. He'd injured his hand on a building site in Cricklewood and the foreman sent him up to the Royal Free. I was working there and bandaged it up for him. He asked me was I free on Saturday and would I meet him in The Gresham. He had nice eyes, and I knew I wouldn't be back to Monaghan for a good while. James and I were never serious. It was just a summer romance, not even a romance, more of a little court."

"So you were never in love with James?"

She threw back her head and laughed.

"Not at all," she said. "If anything it was his brother I liked. He could do card tricks and he'd make you laugh as well. And he was a bit of a buck too."

There was a knock at the door.

"Mary, are you coming?"

"I'll be right out, Jim," she called. "Now, where did I put that present?"

There was a little package standing on the window ledge and I reached up and took it down.

"Is this what you're looking for, Mum?"

"That's it! Now, make sure you patch things up with Mattie before I get back. I'll only be away a wee while. And be a good boy."

She bent down and kissed me on the cheek and was suddenly gone.

That night, in the big double bed we shared, I thought of James and John, and wondered if my father knew about the pair of them. Perhaps that was why he never came on holiday with us, and I fretted a little, and then sleep came in great waves of fog, and I dreamt of letters and card tricks and dribbling past James, John, Rory, Fergus and Mattie to score a wonder goal against the doors of O'Reilly's garage.

And then I dreamt of my mother, and woke in the dark. She wasn't there beside me, and I realised this was the first night we'd ever spent apart. The moon passed by the window, high up in the night sky, trailing clouds and stars. I wondered if she was thinking of me at all and I felt very lonesome for her and thought about James Handley, and wondered if he felt this way when he received her letter, if he'd been able to read what she had said between the lines. The moon withdrew into the night and I turned over in the big empty bed, small and alone and without her.

The Double Corner

had Mattie beat. He was down to his last man and I had two crowns. Another couple of moves and I'd have him. He was edging towards the double corner but that was no odds. I was finally going to nail him.

"Come on, boys. Let's go for a spin."

Uncle Tommy, still in his postman's peaked cap and jacket, his belly hanging out over his baggy trousers, stood at the door. Behind him in the yard the P agus T van rumbled and throbbed as its engine turned over.

"Come on, John Kevin," said Mattie. "We can leave the game till we get back. Mary!"

Mary, stretched out on the settee, looked up from her comic.

"Don't let anyone touch that board!" Mattie barked. "D'you hear?"

"But what if Mammy wants to put out the tea?" asked Mary.

"We'll be back before then," said Uncle Tommy. "Come on, boys, I've some messages to get."

We got up from the table and followed Uncle Tommy out through the back door. The day was warm and sunny, the sky cloudless and blue. Mattie and I crunched on the gravel and I opened the door of the post van. I hopped up onto the black seats, as high off the ground as the saddle of a penny farthing. Mattie landed beside me and then Uncle Tommy got in and took the wheel. He turned his key in the ignition and put his foot on the pedals and we revved off over the gravelled yard and away down the side of the house. He turned left onto the road into Town and I thought about that game of draughts.

"Did you see those goals of Georgie Boy's in England, John Kevin?"

Mattie was football mad. I was too but the difference between us was that I supported West Ham and he supported Manchester United.

"The ones against Benfica?"

"The very ones," said Mattie. "4-1! What a match! Just when they had it won, Eusebio goes and equalises. Busby's dream hangs in the balance… But up steps Georgie, takes the ball around the goalie and in! What a player!"

I thought of the double corner, of how I had Mattie trapped, of how he couldn't shimmy past me and away. My two crowns were bearing down on him like Geoff Hurst and Martin Peters storming towards the German goal. All summer he'd whipped me. Revenge would be sweet. It would be like winning the Jules Rimet Trophy. I tingled with excitement, but said nothing.

We were way past Ballydawn now, the van roaring along. I looked out of the window at the hedgerows passing us by at the side of the road. Uncle Tommy drove steadily, and we were soon rising up on the hill into Town. The outskirts were lined with new bungalows, more every year said my mother, everything changed since she was a girl.

"What have you to get, Daddy?" asked Mattie.

"Ach, a bit of steak, a newspaper, and I need to check if Uncle Mick has sent Auntie Mary over anything."

"Would it be more comics, Daddy?"

"I think it might be something better than comics."

We made our way past the big church to the Diamond and then a little further on and down a side street to the Post Office. We all called it the Post Office, but the sign was in Irish, Post agus Telefoinn, and it made me think about the time Superman was trapped in a parallel world. Ireland was a bit like that. Everything was sort of the same as England, but different, like a draughts board with double corners on the white squares instead of the black ones.

Tommy parked the van outside the grey railings and said, "Hold on there for me, boys. I won't be long."

He turned off down the road. I'd expected him to go into the Post Office to check if my mother had been sent anything, but he must have wanted to get the messages first.

"Who do you think will win the First Division next season, JK?"

"Oh, I don't know, Mattie," I said. "West Ham have some great players –"

"West Ham?!" he snorted. "Would you get away for yourself! How are they going to compete with the likes of Law, Best, Charlton and Kidd?"

"We've got Peters, Moore and Hurst!"

"Sure the only trophy you've ever won has been the Cup Winners' Cup – Man United are European Champions!"

"We've got three World Cup winners in our side," I said. "You've only got one!"

"Who? Charlton? You're forgetting Nobby Stiles! If he didn't do all of Bobby Moore's dirty work for him, you wouldn't have stood a chance!"

"At least we won," I said hotly. "Ireland will never win anything!"

Mattie, his eyes blazing, pushed me. I reeled back and reached for the door handle. I tumbled into the street and he jumped down after me. He rushed forwards and punched me in the stomach. I was winded but mad myself now and I hit him on the arm. He didn't flinch but grabbed my jumper and tried to trip me. I saw it coming and scooped his leg out from under him. He went down and I was on top, pummelling him with my fists. He put his hands up to defend himself, then suddenly, when I thought I had him and he was about to submit, Mattie reached up and got me in a headlock, wrenching me round. One quick punch in the eye and I was done for. Stars lit the back of my head and pain blasted me in bolts of lightning.

"Boys! Boys! Would you stop that?"

Uncle Tommy loomed over us, his great round face like a boxing referee's zooming down to count out the loser. Mattie let go of me, and got up awkwardly. I stayed down, nursing my eye.

"John Kevin," said Tommy, "would you get up out of that?"

"He punched me in the eye," I moaned.

"You say sorry to your cousin!" he barked at Mattie.

"He said Ireland will never win anything!" shouted Mattie.

"What odds!" said Uncle Tommy. "Isn't he a guest in our house?"

"Yes!" I shouted. "A paying guest!"

Tommy and Mattie both roared with laughter and I started to laugh myself. My eye hurt when I laughed but I couldn't help myself. The whole thing was as daft as Dennis The Menace.

"Now are you two going to shake hands and make it up?"

We shook hands and that was an end of it.

Uncle Tommy had a little parcel from the butcher's tucked under his arm and now he unwrapped it and held out the steak on the white paper.

"Here," he said. "Hold this to your eye. It'll stop the bruising."

I put the red marbled meat up to my face. It felt cold and raw. But I was a tough guy now, for all that Mattie had beat me yet again. Wait till we got back and I whipped him at the draughts.

"Now boys," said Tommy. "I've just to go into the Post Office to see if anything has come from Mick. Wait for me in the van – I won't be long."

We hopped back up onto the seats while Tommy walked off to the Post Office. I was still holding up the steak to my eye and starting to feel a bit foolish but it was a quiet day in Town and there was no one around to see me holding a great lump of meat to my face. I was glad. The coolness of the steak was soothing and I wondered if anything had come for me from my father.

"Here he is," said Mattie. "Do you think he has any comics?"

I didn't think so, for it was my mother who sent over the comics, but Uncle Tommy was grinning as he came towards the van. He opened the door and I squinted at him with my one good eye as he stood there in the sunlight.

"Now," he said. "One for your mother, John Kevin, and one for you".

He smiled at me and handed over the letter. I'd never had a letter from my father before.

"Well?" said Mattie. "Aren't you going to open it?"

I was a little afraid of what I might find inside. Uncle Tommy said, "Leave him alone, Mattie. Sure it's nobody's business but his. Now, do you want to give me back my dinner?"

Mattie frowned a little but said nothing as I handed Uncle Tommy back the steak. He wrapped it up in the butcher's paper and walked round to the driver's side.

"We'll be home before you know it now, boys," he said. He placed the parcel of meat on the seat beside him, started up the van and drove off.

We were soon away and rolling along the road to Ballydawn. I started thinking about the game of draughts again, about how I was going to beat Mattie, about how I'd get him back for giving me a black eye.

I never saw the motorbike. The van suddenly took a swerve and the next thing we were dumped in the ditch. Uncle Tommy cursed and Mattie cursed too, but I was too dazed to be angry.

"The bloody fool!" shouted Tommy. "We could have all been killed!"

"What happened?" I asked.

"Some eejit on a motorbike. He shouldn't have been going so fast round that bend! Come on, boys – let's have a look at the damage."

We jumped down from the cab to see that the van's front wheels were stuck in the ridge of the ditch. It looked like a job for International Rescue.

"What'll we do Daddy?" asked Mattie.

"We'll have to walk it," said Tommy. "It's not that far, boys. Then you'll have to take the bike and go back into Town and tell them what's happened. They'll need to tow the van out of the ditch."

"Tommy! Where have you been?"

As we opened the back door five faces looked up at us: Johnny, Geraldine, Evelyn, Mary, and Anna. Auntie Lizzie was by the range. It looked like they'd all had their tea.

"We were run off the road by a mad motorcyclist," said Tommy. "The van's in a ditch about two and a half miles out. Have you anything left for three hungry men?"

Auntie Lizzie served us up some potatoes and cabbage and a bit of cold ham.

"Mary," said Mattie, "where's the draughts?"

"I put the draughts away," said Auntie Lizzie. "They're there under the television."

I looked over at the TV by the far wall. It stood on a shelf under the clock. The draughts set peeped out at me, the game lost forever. Damn! Now I would never beat Mattie. I'd used my best tricks on him, jumping backwards with my crowns, selling one for two, getting in between the middle of a couple of his men. It was all over. I felt sick.

"Hard lines, John Kevin," said Mattie.

I looked at him, but said nothing.

"Where's my mother?" I asked Auntie Lizzie.

"She's having a lie down," she said.

"Thanks," I said. "I think I need one myself."

I went to our room, just to the right of the TV. As I opened the door, I could see that my mother was asleep. I couldn't wake her, even though I wanted to. My eye hurt and so did my pride. I lay down on the bed beside her and let out a sigh.

Then I remembered my father's letter. I reached into my trousers pocket and took it out. I opened the envelope and started to read:

Dear John Boy

I hope you are being a good son to your mother. The weather is very tiresome here of late, with rain and wind most of the time. I hope your own summer is better. I enclose something for you that I hope you will like.

Your Loving Father,

xxx

Three pastel coloured pages fluttered onto the bed. I picked them up and looked at each in turn. It took me a while to work out what they were. They seemed to be just scrawls. But then l looked closer and saw what they said.

"Best wishes, Bobby Moore." "To John, warmest regards, Martin Peters." "For John, Geoff Hurst." I couldn't believe it! My father had sent me the autographs of Bobby Moore, Martin Peters and Geoff Hurst! My favourite players of all time! I felt as if I'd got to the last row of the board and been crowned myself.

I thought of my father then, and hoped the weather might soon be less tiresome for him, and wondered what he'd talked about with Bobby Moore, and Martin Peters, and Geoff Hurst. And I thought of Georgie Best, and wished he could play with them at West Ham, and that one day I'd get his autograph too, and send it in a letter to my father marked P agus T, and wished next year he'd come with so that I didn't miss him, his kind eyes and his soft husky voice, his small, tough hands and his chest as broad as a barrel. I placed the pieces of paper back in the envelope and put it on the bedside cabinet.

In the morning I would take Mattie on again and this time I was going to beat him.

A Visit to Auntie Nora

We turned the corner by the river on the road out of Ballydawn. Queenslough lay on up the other road, and my mother and me set off towards the little scatter of cottages, the sun behind us as we walked together, glad to be out in the warmth, amongst hedgerows and fields and the clear blue sky. There was no one around, only a view of the sawmill about a quarter of a mile ahead of us. A tractor passed by, chugging along on huge wheels, its tyres rutted and clogged with clay.

"Now," said my mother. "We're nearly there. Be sure to be a good boy and say please and thank you."

I told her I would be a good boy and soon we were at Auntie Nora's.

There was a big grey metal gate in front of the cottage and my mother opened it to let us in. She closed it behind her with a clink and we walked up the little path. It was the kind of cottage you heard about in fairy tales, with a bit of thatch on the roof, whitewashed walls, and a well at the side. My mother took me around the back and lifted the latch on the red door. She called into the cottage.

"Hello, Nora! Are you in? It's Mary Murphy come to see you!"

From the front room we could hear someone getting up and walking towards us. A tall woman with a lined face and dark brown hair emerged from the gloom within and opened the door.

"Ach, hello Mary, how are you doing?"

Her voice was full of kindness and warmth, and I felt immediately at home with her. She was my mother's first cousin but my mother called her Auntie Nora and told me that was what I was to call her too. My mother had said that she was a widow, that she had it hard since her husband died ten years ago. She told me that Auntie Nora could be eccentric, that her husband's death had left her a little strange sometimes but to pass no remark. We followed her into the cottage and I saw she was wearing a dark skirt and a green cardigan and had pom poms on her tartan slippers. She turned to me.

"And is this John Kevin? My but you're the big boy now, John Kevin. What age are you?"

"I'm seven," I said.

"Are you, pet? Well come in, come in, and we'll have a little miaow. I haven't much for you, but you're welcome to a cup of tea and a few biscuits for yourself and I might even have a bit of chocolate Swiss Roll. Would you like that, John Kevin?"

"Yes, please," I said. Auntie Nora smiled at me with bright, twinkling eyes. I wondered if they twinkled so much because she was a kind woman, if goodness shone out of a person's eyes, if badness left them dull and hard.

We went into the front room past a wooden table and some straight backed chairs and my mother went and sat down on the settee in front of the fireplace. I sat beside my mother on the settee and Auntie Nora stood in front of us.

"Will you take a cup of tea, Mary? Will I make one for John Kevin?"

"A cup of tea for us would be fine, Nora. Don't trouble yourself too much on our account."

"Ach, sure it's no trouble at all," said Auntie Nora. "Are you over long, Mary?" She walked over to the back of the room, where I could just make out a cage in the dim light, and tapped her fingers on the wire bars.

"We're here till the money runs out or the summer is over," said my mother. "Whichever comes first."

"Pretty Polly! Pretty Polly!"

I jumped a foot. I didn't know birds could talk and the creature startled me. The two cousins laughed when they saw the look on my face.

"Isn't he a fine wee talker, John Kevin?" said Auntie Nora. "He's what you call a mynah bird. He can make any sound he hears, just like an old gramophone."

The kettle whistled in the parlour and she went out to make the tea.

I looked over at the mynah bird. It didn't seem natural, a creature that could talk and make sounds. I wondered if Auntie Nora and her pet ever had conversations, or if he ever tried to fool her by mimicking a knock at the door or a gunslinger saying, "Stick 'em up, lady!" I thought it must be very lonely for her living on her own, with only a bird for company.

"Now," said Auntie Nora. She brought in a tray with cups of tea and biscuits and cake all laid out like a small feast. "Will you come up to the table and we can have a wee ceilidh?"

We went over to the table, and Auntie Nora set out the plates and poured the tea. I noticed that she laid out four plates, but said nothing. My mother had said she could be eccentric and I thought maybe she hadn't counted right.

"There's one for you here too, Mick. Come up to the table and quit footering with that watch, will you?"

I looked around. There was no one else in the room. Auntie Nora seemed to be talking to someone sat in front of the fireplace. I couldn't see anyone. Then my mother kicked me under the table, a sharp blow from the toe of her shoe that made my shin explode with fire and pain. I nearly let out a cry, but she was frowning at me and shaking her head. I was too shocked to speak though. My mother had never kicked me before in my life. I wasn't sure which was the greater hurt, the fire in my shin or the bruise to my heart.

"What's that Mick? You've it nearly working? All right, pet, I'll leave some in the pot till you have it fixed."

She sat down and turned to my mother.

"Honestly, Mary," she said, "he could open a jeweller's with the amount of watches he has."

"Whose watch is he fixing now?" asked my mother.

"JonJo's," said Auntie Nora. "He's been at it this past fortnight, all hunched up, straining at his eyes through that lens of his. But as if he'll listen to me about it."

"Pretty Polly! Pretty Polly!"

The mynah bird hopped around in his cage. He looked like he was enjoying the sport.

I saw now what my mother meant about Auntie Nora. She would have frightened me when I was younger, talking to her dead husband as if he was in the room with her, alive and breathing, instead of in some lonesome graveyard out amongst the drumlins.

Auntie Nora looked at me with her kindly twinkling eyes.

"Of course, you've never met my Mick, have you John Kevin?"

Now she wanted me to take part in her make believe! Usually I was a great one for make believe, out with my pals playing in the street or being cowboys with Mattie down by the river at the back of his house, but pretending to talk to some relative I'd never met who'd been dead for a decade – well, that was asking too much of me.

"Mick, would you say hello to John Kevin?"

"Pretty Polly! Pretty Polly!"

Again my mother kicked me under the table. Why hadn't she warned me about any of this?

"Hello, Uncle Mick," I said.

"Now, John Kevin, would you look at your Uncle, working away on a fine summer's day. I'm sure you won't grow up to ruin your sight under a jeweller's eyepiece like that man of mine. Wait now, pet," said Auntie Nora to me, "and I'll just get that bit of Swiss Roll for you."

She rose out of her chair and went out to the kitchen.

"What's going on?" I asked my mother. Before my mother could reply Auntie Nora returned with the Swiss Roll on a large dish.

"Now," she said, "here's a few slices of cake for you." She carefully placed the slices onto my plate.

I noticed a small grandfather clock by the door to the kitchen.

It looked a little like the one in my uncle's house. I could make out from the hands that the time was one minute to midday, but knew this couldn't be right. We'd set out for Auntie Nora's not long after lunch time, around one o'clock, so it should be nearer two than noon.

"Is your clock not working?" I asked Auntie Nora.

My mother looked mortified. I expected another kick but this time no kick came.

"The clock?" she asked sadly. "That clock stopped working ten years ago. I'm always on at Mick to fix it, but he never will. He won't give me a reason either, just says it'll sort itself out one of these days, that it's just being temperamental. Isn't it funny how he can do all these other timepieces, but he won't touch that clock of ours?"

The two ladies, Auntie Nora and my mother, looked as sad as winter as we sat drinking tea and eating cake.

"Pretty Polly! Pretty Polly!"

Even the mynah bird sounded mournful.

After a while my mother said, "Well, Nora, we must be off now. There's the Murrays to call on as well and I didn't get seeing them yet. Thank you for the lovely tea and cake. We'll be around again before the holidays are over."

She stood up and I stood up with her. Auntie Nora stood too and we were just on the way out when my mother remembered herself.

"Goodbye, Mick," she said. "And good luck with the watches."

I mumbled a farewell and Auntie Nora left us at the door.

"It was lovely seeing you both," she said. "It's been great catching up on old times and meeting young John Kevin here. He's a credit to you."

I couldn't wait to get away and started to fidget.

"Goodbye, Nora," said my mother. "We'll have another ceilidh soon, I promise."

My mother turned and took me by the hand. We went down the path together, opened the gate, and were out onto the road. The sky had clouded over and we walked back to Ballydawn in silence.

The Scholar

ohn, would you like to go to school with your cousins?"

My mother and I were in our room in my aunt and uncle's bungalow. I was lying exhausted on the bed, my mother beside me. It had been a long, tiring journey to my aunt and uncle's house. First there had been the tube to Euston early in the morning, then the train from Euston to Holyhead, then the nightboat to Dun Laoghaire, next the train into Dublin, then the bus to Monaghan, and finally the taxi to Ballydawn. This was the last thing I was expecting.

"But I thought there was no school now?" I said. "I thought we were on holiday?"

"I took you out of school early," said my mother. "Your cousins are still going. To Drumshannon where I went. There's only a week of this summer term left. Why don't you go with them? You might enjoy yourself."

I was quite good at my lessons in London. I liked reading, writing and arithmetic and ever since Miss Riley had brought in chess sets a few weeks ago I had enjoyed watching my classmates play in the afternoon. Miss Riley was brilliant: she stopped doing proper lessons once we'd had afternoon playtime and allowed us to play chess.

I'd brought a little travelling chess set with me to Ireland and I was looking forward to teaching Mattie. And beating him. I'd got one of those Know The Game books and had been reading it on the journey and practising a few moves. I particularly liked pins and forks and skewers and the Ruy Lopez.

"Do they play chess at Drumshannon?" I asked my mother.

"I don't know," she said. "But they might let you teach them."

That decided it. I would go to Drumshannon with my cousins in the morning and introduce my classmates to chess.

"What do you do at school in London, John Kevin?"

Evelyn walked beside me, the rest up ahead. It was three miles' walk to school and I'd had to get up early, snatch at my breakfast with the rest of my cousins, and set off. I don't think I'd ever walked three miles in my life before. My travelling chess set was in my duffle bag and I felt like an explorer.

The early morning sun was shining, and the hedges along Clintock's Lane caught the light on the leaves, a flickering show of yellow and green as we walked along. Geraldine, Mattie, Mary, and Anna were all ahead of us. There was no Johnny as he was finishing his first year at the Tech, and had set off the other way into town with Uncle Tommy in the car.

"Well," I said, thinking about Miss Riley. "We haven't really done much except play chess."

"Chess, John Kevin? That's a funny subject to be studying at school. Is that not just a game?"

"It is a game, Evelyn, but it's much more than that as well."

I told her about the maharajahs, about them playing to stop warring with each other, about my theory that it was actually all *about* them warring with each other, but I could see Evelyn wasn't really getting it. She needed to see the board, the pieces and the pawns, to try a few moves. It was a pretty abstract game at the best of times – you couldn't understand the personalities of the chessmen (was the Queen a chessman?) without seeing them, touching them, moving them.

"Do you think they'd let me show you how to play at school?" I asked.

By now we'd nearly got to the end of Clintock Lane. The sun was getting warmer and as we passed Mrs Kelly's cottage and started to come out onto the road for Drumshannon I could feel the heat make my face blush.

"I'm not sure about that, John Kevin. You could try. But I think you'll find the lads prefer hopping a ball around to moving wee men across a board."

Miss McKenna stood in front of the class.

"Who made you?"

"God made me."

"Why did God make you?"

"God made me to know Him, love Him and serve Him in this world, and be happy with Him forever in the next."

We all sang out the Catechism as if we were chanting our times tables. Miss McKenna was a dark-haired young woman in an Aran cardigan with brown leather buttons, a blue flowery blouse, pleated tartan skirt, and black tights. She wore brown brogues with flat heels, and looked much more severe than Miss Riley.

"To whose image and likeness did God make you?"

"God made me to his own image and likeness."

I was surprised that there was no difference in the Catechism we learnt in London. But then this was the Catholic Church and I wondered if the Pope played chess and who would be a match for him? My mother said he knew everything. He must be unbeatable. He was the King on a huge worldwide chessboard, with lots of bishops, and castles, and knights of the Church. And I was just a little pawn, one of millions.

"John Kevin, how many pennies are there in five shillings?"

I froze. I had been daydreaming again, about chess, and the worldwide game the Pope played against the Forces of Darkness. The question about pennies made me panic. Everybody was looking at me, the English boy from London.

"Sixty!"

A voice from behind hissed the answer.

"Sixty," I said.

Miss McKenna looked at me. Her eyes seemed to harden, to bore right into my own.

"And how did you arrive at that answer?"

I was trapped. I couldn't say someone told me. I would get them into trouble. Instead of Miss McKenna I'd have the whole class against me.

"I guessed," I said.

Everybody was quiet. But I wasn't going to own up. I couldn't. I was going to have to try and bluff it out.

"Guessed?" said Miss McKenna.

Now there was a tension in the air that felt like it was going to explode. As I started to turn cold the door opened and in walked a man in a black suit. Everyone was suddenly standing.

"Good morning Fr McCabe."

I was still sitting down in my seat, mesmerised by Miss McKenna, the arrival of Fr McCabe, what would happen next.

Fr McCabe caught my eye. He had the same cold look I'd seen in Miss McKenna's stare. Now there were two of them.

"Good morning, children. Please sit down."

My classmates sat down again and I sighed with relief. It looked like I was going to get away with it.

Fr McCabe walked over to my desk.

"And what is your name, my son?" he said.

"John, Father," I answered.

"Stand up!" he barked.

I rose from my chair. If anything the atmosphere in the room had grown even more tense.

"Have you no manners, you little blackguard?" he snarled. "When anyone comes into class you're supposed to stand up. Like everyone else. Or didn't you see them, you cur? Miss McKenna, who is this boy? I've never seen him before. Is he some tinker's child, or what?"

"Father, this is Matthew Murphy's cousin, over from England. I asked him the answer to a sum. Instead of giving me an answer himself or telling me he didn't know he waited for someone to tell him."

Fr McCabe never took his eyes off me.

"And *did* someone tell him, Miss McKenna?"

"They did, Father."

"And has his accomplice owned up? Or has he identified them?"

"He has not."

"I see," said Fr McCabe with a cold finality. "I am aware, Miss McKenna, that you will be letting these little ruffians out to play in five minutes. I came here in the hope that I might catch them all hard at work. Instead I find duplicity and insufferable disrespect. Miss McKenna, I think when you have gone to have your morning cup of tea with your colleagues I should like to keep the class behind. A few decades of the rosary are called for. Until then, Miss McKenna, I shall let you carry on with your lesson."

Fr McCabe continued to stand over me. Miss McKenna went round the class, asking them all questions about pounds, shillings, and pence, about how long it would take two men to dig a hole four foot wide and six foot deep, then how long it would take four men to dig the same hole, or six men, or how long it would take to travel from Dublin to Galway at a speed of sixty miles an hour, or how many apples you could buy for thirty shillings if apples weighed an average of six ounces and you could buy them for a shilling a pound. She asked everyone a question except me. And all the while Fr McCabe stood over me until the bell rang. Miss McKenna excused herself, then Fr McCabe made us all kneel on the hard parquet floor and recite two decades of the Rosary. I thought my knees were going to crack. And then she came back.

Fr McCabe gave me that same cold hard look before he spun on his heel and opened the classroom door, bid Miss McKenna goodbye and was gone. She ordered us back to our seats, all of us rubbing our knees as we sat back down, and then started talking in a language I had never heard before.

It was Irish, and the next hour passed even more terrifyingly than the last. For I started imagining that Miss McKenna was talking about me, knowing full well I couldn't understand a word she was saying. I imagined she was telling my classmates what an insufferable boy I was, what a blackguard, what a knave. I felt them all looking at me, but continued to look straight ahead, as if none of this was going on, as if Miss McKenna and my classmates, the class itself, the very school, didn't exist.

And then the bell rang and it was time for lunch.

A car passed me on the road, but I kept my head down and carried on walking.

By now I reckoned Miss McKenna had phoned the police, that the next car I heard would be the Guards, but I just kept on. What else could I do? I wasn't playing truant – I was on holiday, and they couldn't make me go back.

Could they?

I started running, my duffle bag hitting against my back, the little chessmen rattling in the Travelling Chess set. But I didn't care about chess now – I just wanted to get back to my mother.

"John!"

My mother had been having a nap, lying on our bed fast asleep. I'd stood watching her for a few moments until some change in the room made her realise I was there.

"Don't send me back!" I cried. "Miss McKenna hates me! Fr McCabe hates me! And all of the other children hate me as well!"

I flung myself on the bed and started sobbing. She took hold of me and lifted my head up by the chin.

"What happened?" she asked.

I told her all about Miss McKenna's question about how many pennies there were in five shillings, about the voice behind me giving me the answer, about Fr McCabe coming in, about the names he called me, about him making us say the Rosary on the hard floor, the nightmare of it all, of me running down the road, afraid the police might catch me and bring me back.

"Oh dear!" she said. "And I thought you might like to see out the week in Drumshannon. What are we going to do with you?"

I started crying then. I thought I couldn't get out of it, that somehow I would have to go back again tomorrow.

"Please don't send me back!" I begged, lunging for her, needing her embrace, the warmth of her.

"There, there," she said, patting me on the back. "Don't worry.

Sure they won't miss you, anyway." She laughed then, and I could feel my face reddening. "God, John, but you're a real scholar!"

I wasn't sure if she was praising me or not. But at least I didn't have to go back to Drumshannon. I felt like a pawn that had got to the end of the board.

Now where was that book about chess?

A Bike Ride

Mattie and I swung out on the bikes. We took off onto the road and away.

"We'll go as far as Hollywood. Come on."

Mattie rose in the saddle, cowboy style, and shot ahead of me. I almost thought he was going to give it a crack on the flanks and yell, "Hi ho, Silver! Away!" I stood up on the pedals myself and pulled in behind him, the day warm on my back and the neighbours' hedges full of sweet country smells, woodsmoke and leaves and grass still moist with dew.

The village rolled away behind me, the white bungalows and green hedges disappearing with every revolution of the sit-up-and-beg's wheels. The bike was too big for me, but Mattie's was even bigger – and his had a crossbar too. But that didn't bother Mattie – he was able for any yoke. And he could dismount by scooting along with both feet on the one pedal. I had to pull her in and get off carefully. They could be dangerous things, bikes.

We passed the creamery, clanking and hammering away, and crossed the bridge to Ballydawn, the cottages and cluster of shops, O'Reilly's garage, the green and cream telephone box on the road out to Scottsville.

"Do you know Hollywood?"

"Is that where they make the films?"

Mattie laughed.

"That's in America, you eejit. There's a lake there and we're going to swim it."

"But we have no togs!"

"Who needs them on a day like this?"

We came to the old church at the top of the hill, and Mattie put his feet up on the handlebars. He was freewheeling now, down to Jameson's farm and the pond at the bottom of the hill, daredevilling along on the bike's big wheels. I was freewheeling myself, but I hung on to the handlebars, grim and determined. It was just like riding the wind. The air rushed past my ears and I felt at the mercy of the big awkward machine as I flew down the hill. At last I came to the bottom and the rise eventually levelled out, the bikes' slower, calmer now, as we passed the flat, quiet fields that lay either side of the road to Scottsville.

There wasn't a car to be seen and the sky was as blue as the ocean, cloudless and still. Above the wide open heavens in outer space rockets were travelling to the moon and sputniks orbited mysteriously. It made me dizzy looking up at the endless miles and thinking about how far it was to the moon, to the stars.

"Keep in!" yelled Mattie. A motorbike roared up behind, and startled the bejaysus out of me. I swerved into the ditch, fell off the big machine and lay with it on top, a wheel still spinning and my legs and elbows badly skinned.

Mattie looked down at me.

"What kind of eejit are you?"

I blushed scarlet, flustered and ashamed of myself.

"Get up out of that," he said. "Are you all right?"

I wasn't, but I nodded.

"Let's go."

Mattie was away before I could even get the bike out of the ditch. I mounted it as quickly as I could and set off after him.

We rode on in silence for another half hour. The road was straight and level and the going easy, the bikes flying along and the day bright and sunny. I forgot about my shins and my elbow, and started to relax in the warmth and sunshine.

"Not long now," called Mattie as we passed a sign that read "Hollywood ¼".

We cycled along and Mattie let me catch up and ride side by side with him. The road narrowed to a lane and we rolled into Hollywood. Up ahead I could see an open expanse of land and the lake appeared, a large flat mirror, silver and blue, with not a soul in sight.

"Come on," said Mattie, and he dismounted in that cool cowboy way of his, scooting along until he pulled the critter up short.

I stopped my bike a little behind him and got off as carefully as I could. Even without a crossbar, I was high up on the saddle and didn't want to scuff and scar myself any more than I'd done already.

We laid our bikes by the edge of the lake and Mattie started to take off his clothes. He wasn't a bit embarrassed, standing naked and proud in the sunshine. I was a lot slower about undressing.

"What are you waiting for?" he demanded. "Sure we haven't all day. This place will fill up with all sorts of jossers any minute. If you don't hurry up they'll see us."

I pulled off my y-fronts. Mattie grinned, turned and ran into the lake. I followed and we swam towards the opposite shore, about a hundred yards or so, Mattie going like a torpedo, like an Olympic champion. I breast-stroked in his wake, knowing I couldn't match him for technique or power.

He came to the shallows at the far side of the water and turned onto his back, floating in the still calm lough. I pulled up alongside him.

"Not a bit cold, is it?" said Mattie. I thought it was cold enough, but I just grinned.

"Not a bit," I said.

"I'll race you back," he said. "You take a five yard start. The loser gets the ice creams."

I swam the five yards ahead. Mattie stood smiling in the water as I looked round at him. That five yards seemed quite a distance and I started to fancy my chances.

"You start us off," I called back to him.

"All right," he said. "On your marks, get set…"

But before I heard the word "Go!" a great splash told me that

Mattie had hit the water and was away. I kicked off and started piling the lakewater behind me, the world a blur of surf and spray as I thrashed and hauled myself through the green lough.

I was still ahead after fifty yards, but only just. Mattie was like a rocket, like a missile, and I could feel him gaining on me. I urged myself on, determined not to give up without a fight, but it was no good. Slowly, ruthlessly, he was starting to catch me up. I thought of the legend of The Red Hand Of Ulster, the bloody claw hacked off and thrown at the shore to claim the land. In that moment, Mattie overtook me, and I knew I'd be getting the ice creams.

He ploughed on ahead, stroke after stroke taking him further and further away from me, till he was just a few feet from where we'd started. Winded now, and well beaten, I gave up the race to him. He deserved his winnings.

"The champion!" he cried, arms aloft, standing in the shallow water at the lake's edge. "That's a big slider you owe me!"

I came panting through the shallows and stopped a few yards from him. I wasn't about to roll over completely.

"But you started before you were supposed to!" I cried. "You cheated!"

"Just because you didn't hear me shout "Go!" doesn't mean to say I didn't! You're just being a bad loser!"

"On no I'm not!"

"Oh yes you are!"

Mattie started chucking water, splashing me in torrents. I gave as good as I got, splashing him back, but he was getting the better of me.

"All right, all right!" I cried. "You win!"

"So you're going to get me that slider?"

Hostilities ceased.

"Yes," I said.

"A big one?"

"A great big one," I said.

Mattie grinned at me in triumph. He skipped out of the lake and ran towards the place where we had thrown down our clothes and left the bikes. I followed him and we started drying ourselves on our shirts and getting dressed. My clothes stuck and clung to my wet flesh and I had to pull hard at my pants, shorts, and socks to get them on. Mattie didn't seem to be having any trouble. In next to no time he was dressed and dry.

We lay side by side, the warm day and the race leaving me relaxed and peaceful. The view of the cloudless sky was worth any slider. I was lost in thoughts of ice cream when Mattie said quietly,

"Do you remember Auntie Annie?"

A dragonfly hovered over the lake before shooting off across it like a small gaudy jet.

"Yes," I said.

"Do you remember playing up on her farm?"

"I do."

"And do you remember that big white horse she had?"

I smiled and nodded.

"That horse lived to be older than she did," said Mattie. "Poor Auntie Annie."

Mattie spoke quietly, his cowboy bravura gone now.

"Daddy took it bad. I remember going to visit her in Dublin, in the hospital. The smell of the place. A smell of medicine, only worse, and the size of it. Mammy and Daddy and the rest of us went down one day to see her. She was terribly failed, her red hair white then. That was a big shock. It made her look old. And she'd grown a hump on her back. She smiled at us, but we all knew she wouldn't last long. Leukaemia. A terrible way to go. Your blood is poisoned and you can't fight off illness. Sure a cold would kill you."

Mattie fell silent and I saw his eyes turn inward. It was as if he was talking to himself, as if I wasn't there.

"The telegram came on a Monday morning to the Post Office. Daddy was given leave and had to make the arrangements. Your mother came over. How did she get the news?"

I thought of that night, of my mother crying, of the week I spent with my father.

"The Higginses came to the door," I said. "We'd all gone to bed, and I remember the knock made me jump. We didn't have a telephone, but they did. They drove over to tell us. My mother

56

knew as soon as she heard them at the door. She let them in and just broke down."

As I spoke, two swifts appeared, circling and swooping overhead.

"She was at the wake," he said. "Your mother and my father gave out The Rosary. And the house was full all the time. There were people at the door every five minutes. 'Sorry for your trouble,' they all said. I passed no remark, though I thought it a strange thing to say – 'trouble' was just too small a word for what happened to Auntie Annie."

So this was what my mother had gone through. I thought when she came back home to us that she'd changed, that my aunt's death had taken something from her. She had lost some of her spirit, I thought. It was gone in longing and grief and I wondered if it would ever come back to her.

"Come on," said Mattie, suddenly jumping up. "I'll take you to the grave and we can say a prayer."

He took up his bike and was away. I followed behind, and we cycled the half mile over to the chapel where Auntie Annie was buried. We left our bikes at the side of the church and Mattie led me through the rows of graves to a plain white wooden cross.

"There she is," said Mattie.

On the cross was written, 'Anne Murphy 1939 – 1968'. I looked at the cross and tried to take thirty-nine away from sixty-eight, but got confused putting back the one. Mattie blessed himself and said a silent prayer.

"Come on," he said.

We walked back to the bikes and I thought, as Mattie, mounted his yoke, that I could see a small tear at the corner of his eye, but I said nothing, and followed him out of the churchyard and down all the country roads back home, his back to me all the way, wondering now if he'd forgotten about that slider.

Translation

'm Irish," I said.

"No you're not," said Rory McDermott. "But we can make an Irishman out of you."

"But I *am* Irish!"

"You're English, boy, there's no two ways about that. But if you want we have the way of turning Sassenachs into Paddies."

I turned to Mattie but he looked away and I knew I was on my own.

"All right then," I said, "what do I have to do?"

"Now up here," said Rory, "there's a fairy fort. This is where you have to go through the first part of the Translation."

We came to a clearing in the woods. Dusk had started to fall, and the ghost of a pale moon hung in the sky. I could see a small mound ahead and we walked towards it.

"And what do I have to do?" I asked.

"Now the first part," said Rory, "is all about renouncing your place of birth. In order to do this, you have to strip naked."

"Strip naked!" I shouted. "In front of you lot?!"

"Not just in front of us," said Fergus seriously. "In front of the little people as well."

"You're kidding me," I said.

"Do you want to stay a Sassenach?" asked Rory. "Or do you want to become one of us?"

I searched their faces, Mattie's as well. They all looked as serious as a conclave of cardinals. Not a giggle or a titter, not so much as a smile between them.

"But why do I have to be naked?"

"Being naked symbolises leaving behind your old Sassenach self. You are about to start a process of rebirth." Rory, twelve and taller than the rest of us, gazed steadily into my face. What he said sounded demented, but it made a kind of mad, moonlit sense too.

"And then what do I do?" I asked.

"Then you have to dance round the fairy fort three times."

"Three times?"

"Yes, said Rory.

"And how will I know it's gone OK?"

"The fairies will let us know," said Fergus.

"Oh yes?" I asked, sceptical as hell now. "And will they let me know too?"

"Only Irish people – *real* Irish people – can see the fairies," said Fergus hotly. "Only real Irish people can hear them. When you have performed the first part of the Translation correctly, pronouncing the spell and doing the dance, if the fairies approve they will sing a special fairy song in acknowledgement."

I looked him in the eye. Nothing, not a flicker.

"So when I've done all this I'll be able to see and hear the fairies myself?"

"Of course," answered Fergus.

I stood there, weighing it all up.

"Well," said Mattie, "are you going to do it, or what?"

Even my cousin was against me.

I started to take off my clothes slowly, as slowly as I could. I got down to my vest and pants and stopped.

"What are you waiting for?" urged Mattie. "Do you want to be one of our own or don't you?"

Reluctantly, I took off my vest and slowly pulled down my pants.

Ireland was a strange place. Last year my mother had had the shingles. When she went to the doctor in London he gave her powder for it. My cousin Geraldine told me she had had the shingles too. But there was no powder to soothe her. On the first night of the full moon she was taken to a farm, where a chicken had its throat cut. As the blood spurted it was splashed on her bare chest and back. She was cured in an instant.

"Do I have to say anything?" I asked.

"You have to say: I curse the land that gave me birth, of all the lands upon the earth. And you have to say it three times, don't forget." Rory looked at me sternly.

It was hard to guess what he was thinking. He might be bluffing, but then where had he got the rhyme from? He'd have to be quick to think that one up.

I wasn't so slow myself.

"Clockwise or anti-clockwise?"

"Anti-clockwise," said Fergus.

I looked at them again.

Nothing.

They could have been marble.

I started to jig slowly around the mound, feeling peculiar and foolish, my hands covering my private parts, aware of their deadpan faces, their eyes upon me, reciting the spell as I went: "I curse the land that gave me birth, of all the lands upon the earth."

"Well?" I asked when I had finished. "Did I get it right?"

"You did," said Fergus.

"Come on," said Rory. "You've the river to swim next."

I trudged through the woods, still naked, the other boys carrying my clothes. Rory told me that I wasn't allowed to touch anything I'd worn until the whole Translation had been carried out. I was starting to get used to being naked though. Even if they were putting me on, at least I was getting somewhere. I was showing the rest that I could take being stripped and marched and manipulated. It seemed as good a way as any to prove how Irish I was.

"Right," said Rory. "Here we are."

He stood where the riverbank meandered through the trees and a blackbird sang overhead somewhere up in the forest's canopy.

Moonlight oozed into the river and we all gazed on the silver water.

"For the second part of the Translation," said Fergus, "you have to swim from one side of the river to the other three times. You have to say as you do this: I swim the stream to be reborn, to light into a bright new dawn."

"What do I do about getting out?" I asked.

"Just hop onto the bank of the river," said Fergus.

I smelt a rat.

"What – on the other side?" I said. "What about you lot? How am I going to meet you? If I swim backwards and forward three times I'll end up on the bank opposite you all."

Fergus didn't miss a beat.

"We'll walk along this side of the riverbank, till we get to the bridge. You cross over and meet us, and then you have only one more part of the Translation left."

My resistance was disappearing with the fading light. I looked from one member of the gang to the other. The darkness deepened another shade and only their eyes gave any clue to what they were thinking. But I couldn't read them. They looked as serious as ever.

I looked down into the stream. Its moonlit depths gave nothing away either. Whatever was on the other side of the river, whatever lay beyond, whether 'Translation' or just a bit of sport, I was going to know soon. I waded in. The water was as cold as the vast wastes of space and soon my teeth were chattering.

"Don't forget the blessing!" shouted Fergus.

"What is it?" I shouted back, kicking off for the other side.

"I swim the stream to be reborn, to light into a brighter dawn!"

"That's not what you said the first time!" I shouted back.

I was about halfway now, the river's current flowing against me, carrying me further downstream.

"You have it wrong, Fergus!" cried Rory. "It's: I swim the stream to be reborn, to light into a bright new dawn."

Now I really did suspect that they were having me on. But having come this far what would be the point of turning back?

I swam through the moonlit water, imagining it to be some magical element, quicksilver, fairydew, dragon's blood. I started reciting the rhyme as I neared the far bank, trying to make the words sound out strong through my chattering teeth.

"I swim the stream to be reborn, to light into a bright new dawn!"

I must have looked a right fool, but again, in that river, at that moment, with the moon high up above and the stream pushing against me as I swam, I felt I *was* being translated, that I was proving to Mattie and the boys that I was as Irish as them if not more so.

At the second crossing I started getting used to the coldness. My teeth stopped chattering and the world around me settled into a hush, the only sound the splashing of my arms and legs through the water and a blackbird singing up above me. I touched the riverbank nearest the boys, and turned round immediately without looking at them, crying out once more the rhyme: "I swim the stream to be reborn, to light into a bright new dawn!"

With a just a few more strokes I would be at the far side again, and the second part of my translation would be complete.

Suddenly, a long dark streak of muscle shot past. I froze as the creature stopped and turned. Two submerged eyes took a bead on me. Whatever it was I didn't like the look of it. I started kicking and crashing as hard as I could towards the riverbank. The creature – an otter? an eel? a monster? – started chasing me. The boys on the riverbank had seen what was happening and were all shouting:

"Don't forget the rhyme!"

"You have to say it a third time before you can get out of the river!"

"Watch out!"

In my cold terror I couldn't remember the words. The creature was gaining on me. I was close to panicking. Supposing it bit me? Sunk me? Ate me?!!! From the bank behind, whoops suddenly split the night. I turned round to see the creature gone, splashes in my wake. It was Rory and Mattie, firing stones into the river. Fergus must have downed the beast, for he punched the air like a boxer who'd won the world championship, and did a little jig on the riverbank.

I felt exhilarated. I shouted out the rhyme in triumph, the

words coming back to me in a rush of relief as I stretched for the riverbank.

"I swim the stream to be reborn, to light into a bright new dawn!"

"Well done, John Kevin!" shouted Mattie. "You've only the last task left!"

I crossed over to the other side of the bridge. In front of me stood Rory, Fergus and Mattie. The water from the stream was cooling on my skin and I knew that my teeth would start chattering again soon.

"Can I put on my clothes now?" I asked.

"Not until the final part of the Translation is complete," said Rory. "Come on. You're nearly an Irishman! Only one more task to perform!"

They all turned and set off through the woods, and I followed behind. My bare shoeless feet hurt with each step as twigs and stones and leaves left their mark on me, but I pressed on, determined now to see it through. Even if they had been joking me, I'd show them that I was tough enough to suffer whatever they'd dreamed up. And if it *was* all a joke, well, I'd take it in good part, and leave them shamefaced, for they'd be the ones getting into trouble, not me.

We came to a path, the ground suddenly less broken and various. Up ahead I could see where the woods petered out. Through a gap in the trees a large building stood silhouetted against the night, and I knew we were at Ballyshannon Chapel.

"What are we doing here? I asked.

"We're not doing anything," replied Fergus. "It's you's the one who's doing, not us."

"OK. So what comes next?"

It was night now, the black sky like a cloth of velvet for the biggest pearliest moon I"d ever seen.

"Your ancestors," said Rory, "are buried in that chapel's graveyard. It's only from them that you can be made into an Irishman. From them and St Patrick."

"You lot must think I'm crazy!"

They'd gone too far. Fun was fun, but this was getting scary.

"What are you saying?" asked Mattie quietly. "Are you saying that we would make mock? That we'd bring you to the chapel just to have you commit a sacrilege? I thought you knew us better than that."

Mattie was an altar server. It always amazed me how such a scut changed on stepping across the threshold of the chapel. As soon as that holy water hit him, he was like a saint entering heaven.

I paused. Then I said, "OK. So what am I supposed to do?"

"You're to go into that churchyard. You know where your grandfather and your grandmother are buried? Well, you must go to their graves and say the following, St Patrick, St Patrick, hear what I say, O make me Irish in every way."

They were serious. There was more gravity amongst the three of them than there was holding up the stars in the heavens.

"All right," I said. "Give me my clothes."

"No clothes," said Fergus. "You only get them when you've done it."

"You must think I'm mad!" I said. "Prancing around in a graveyard in the dead of night completely starkers! Are you trying to make a monkey out of me?"

"A monkey?" asked Mattie. "No, John Kevin – we want to make an Irishman out of you. All through this whole thing you've been kicking up a fuss about what we've said you have to do. I'm not sure you really mean what you say. It seems as if being brought up in England has turned you against us. Do you not like us? Is that it? Do you feel you need to look down on us? Are we not good enough for you?"

"No," I said, "that's not what I think at all."

"Well what is it?" asked Mattie. "Why are you so against all of this? Do you not trust us? If you can't trust us, how can you be one of us?"

"It's not me who's in the wrong here," I said hotly. "It's you. If you really trusted me, you would have taken me at my word: I *am* Irish. But if that's not good enough for you, then watch this."

I jumped up onto the churchyard wall and clambered over. I

landed on the other side, my shins skinned, but picked myself up. I was angry now, and though it felt kind of spooky to be wandering around amongst the gravestones at the dead of night, any fear or embarrassment, any reservations I had, were burnt up to pieces by my desire to show the three of them.

I headed off for the corner of the churchyard where my grandparents were buried when I heard the sound of running feet. I froze, straining to hear what was happening. Then came the heavier tread of footsteps towards me.

"What in God's Holy Name have we here?"

It was Fr Ryan, coming through a row of graves, a dark shape in the moonlit churchyard. I was mortified. I had no clothes on, and, I could see now, no excuse to be standing transfixed in front of him. I realised that the running feet I'd heard were my accomplices scooting off into the night. I'd been abandoned, and the whole 'Translation' lark had been one big con. I was well and truly had. The only Translation I'd undergone was from boy to fool. I blushed with anger and shame as the priest marched toward me.

"My God!" he said as he made me out in the darkness. "Where are your clothes, my son?"

"Halfway to Ballydawn, Father."

"What? What are you talking about?"

I told him what had happened, how I'd been tricked, how sorry I was feeling.

He started laughing then, and I knew I wasn't in half the trouble I thought I was.

"We'd better clothe your nakedness," he said, chuckling away. "Come on in to the presbytery. They might not have made an Irishman out of you, my son, but by God, you're game. Wait till Fr Casey hears about this."

I could see I was going to be a laughing stock. My name would be mud all over the parish and beyond. But what could I do?

We walked in silence until we came to the far side of the church where the presbytery stood. As Fr Ryan stepped up to the door, I said, "Father, once I've got something on me, could I ask you something?"

"Yes, my son?" he replied, taking the key out of his pocket and fitting it in the lock.

"All this, Father, the immodesty, the graveyard – will you hear my confession?

Fr Ryan turned back to look at me. The door was open now and I could see into the darkness of the hallway. It was pitch black, but I could tell by the silence that passed between us that Fr Ryan was giving me what's called an old-fashioned look. I had him. The night's events would remain sealed in the confessional. He could tell no one once I'd fessed up. And the boys could tell no one either, otherwise there'd be a whole heap of trouble. And if they ever mentioned it to me, I'd drop them all in it.

I followed Fr Ryan inside and although I dared not laugh, I was grinning the broadest grin of my life. For faintly, on a light breeze that whispered through the door closing behind me, I thought I heard the fairies singing, and for the first time during that very long night I felt at last at home.

Dust to Dust

We stood in the sacristy and waited for Fr Ryan. The smell of beeswax and lingering incense hung in the air, and I thought hungrily of the breakfast I would eat after serving Mass.

"He's getting late," said my cousin.

Suddenly the door from the presbytery opened and in walked Fr Casey, portly, frowning and red-faced, the broken veins in his cheeks like a map of Hell's rivers.

"Is Fr Ryan not coming, Father?" asked Mattie.

"No," answered Fr Casey gruffly. "Mrs Murray sent her eldest boy up on the bike about half an hour ago. Her husband is in a bad way and needs a priest. I had to send Fr Ryan."

Mattie and I looked at each other. Fr Casey's young curate was a much nicer priest to serve Mass for altogether, according to my cousin. He wouldn't scold you on the altar or give you a telling off back in the sacristy when it was over. Mattie said Fr Casey was fond of a drop of the hard stuff, "a strong man's failing", but Fr Casey didn't look strong this morning. He was suffering, his face ruby from the booze, cranky as a hornet in a bottle.

"Well come on," he barked. "We'd better get it over with."

Uncle Seamus's ashes stood on the dresser behind us, a whole shoebox of them. I'd never heard of anyone being cremated before. Uncle Seamus had emigrated to America when he was a young man and had died in New York a fortnight ago, aged 69. He was my mother's uncle and wanted to be buried back in Ballydawn. But he had no family out in America: he'd never married and there was no one who would pay for his body to be shipped back home. So it was decided that he should be cremated and his ashes sent over. My mother told me that the Pope had just allowed cremation for Catholics although I didn't fancy it myself. How could you be resurrected from ashes blown about everywhere on the wind?

It was a poor way to go. But this was to be his Requiem and Mattie and I were not about to let anybody down. Seamus wanted a day we'd all remember, according to his friend Mr Lupelli, who lived in Queens. My mother had shown me the letter, and I'd marvelled at the stamp. It showed Colonel John Glenn splashing down, and I wondered if we'd ever send letters to the moon and how much the stamps would cost.

"Hurry up!" said Fr Casey. "It's time to get ready."

His hands trembled as we helped him into his vestments, and I knew this wasn't going to be easy. When we were done he said,

"Are those the ashes?"

"Yes, Father," said Mattie.

"Come on then," said the priest. Fr Casey picked up the box of Uncle Seamus's remains and processed solemnly with them out to the altar. Mattie and I followed behind.

The chapel was full to bursting. I recognised my mother, my aunt and uncle and my cousins, all in their Sunday Best sitting in the front pew to the right of the altar. There were a few other relatives I knew dotted about amongst the congregation, then a whole sea of faces I didn't know at all. The turnout meant that at least Uncle Seamus was getting a good send-off.

Mattie and I followed Fr Casey to the altar, and stood either side of him. The priest put the box of ashes on the altar, bowed, and welcomed everyone. I noticed the statues were all covered, but was still a little lightheaded from the overnight fast to take much notice. I knew I had to concentrate on getting everything right. Fr Ryan had granted special permission for me, as Uncle Seamus's grand-nephew, to serve Mass. Although this was the One, Holy, Catholic And Apostolic Church, the universal church throughout the world,

I thought there might be some little differences in the way Mass was said here, and that if I wasn't on my toes, so to speak, I might make some terrible mistake, like getting my responses wrong, or, God forbid, dropping the chalice or spilling the wine. I wanted to fit in, not make a show of myself.

But it was going well. The Kyrie was out of the way and Mattie and I went to the opposite ends of the altar and sat in the choirstalls for the Readings. My mother took the second reading, from St Paul's First Letter To The Corinthians. I wasn't sure who the Corinthians were, but I knew that footballers in Queen Victoria's time were named after them. Mr O'Reilly, who took us for RE, said St Paul was a good runner and I wondered if he played football up in heaven with the Corinthians.

I started to daydream. I often did when I was hungry and I had a hunger on me now that made me dream of fry ups, and stews and dumplings. I was ready to eat a carthorse and I'd moved on from wondering about how Uncle Seamus had got to know Mr Lupelli to thinking about New York and cheeseburgers and thick strawberry milkshakes when I heard Fr Casey hissing at me.

"Give me the ashes!"

I jumped a foot. Why did Fr Casey want Uncle Seamus's ashes? Surely there was a good bit of the Mass still to go?

"Come on you young pup, what are you waiting for?"

Fr Casey's red-rimmed eyes were boring into me. He was not a man to be crossed, especially at 10am on a dreary midweek morning, suffering the horrors, full of fire and brimstone. I stepped out from the choirstall and advanced to the altar. I picked up the box containing Uncle Seamus's ashes, walked over to Fr Casey and handed them to him

He gave me a dirty look from his glassy eyes. I nodded reverently and returned to the choirstall. By now I was thoroughly puzzled. Shouldn't Mass be entering the holy moments of prayer and transubstantiation I had witnessed countless times, knew almost backward from having served on the altar in England? I thought perhaps I had missed something, that my daydreaming had led to me skipping great passages of this Requiem, Uncle Seamus's farewell to the gleaming towers of downtown Manhattan, to modern times and the future, to Ballydawn and where he'd come from.

Slowly, the congregation approached the altar rails. Fr Casey was there to greet them, a small metal vessel in his hands. As each parishioner approached him, he put his thumb in the vessel and placed the sign of the cross on their foreheads. My mother was the first to receive Fr Casey's blessing and as she turned away I was mortified.

There, on her forehead, was a smear of ash. I knew now why the statues were veiled: this was Ash Wednesday, the start of Lent, and all the people processing up to receive the sign of the cross were being smudged with ashes from the box on the altar. Fr Casey had decanted them into his little vessel and was signalling now for me to come and top him up. But the ashes were the wrong ashes! The ashes in the box were the remains of Uncle Seamus! They weren't the ashes for Ash Wednesday at all!

What I could I do? I couldn't stop the Mass. Fr Casey would excommunicate me. From the choirstall opposite Mattie was grinning like a cat, but I didn't think it was a laughing matter, not at all. Fr Casey was looking very cross now. He must be running out, I realised, and there were still lots of people needing their ashes.

I walked over to the altar, bowed and picked up the box of Uncle Seamus's remains. I took the box to Fr Casey, who used a little scoop to decant them into his vessel. I bowed and walked back to the choirstall, as the priest continued applying Uncle Seamus's ashes to the foreheads of the mourners. I was powerless to stop him, resigned now to Fr Casey dispersing the last of Uncle Seamus onto the foreheads of the congregation, and watched as they all walked solemnly back down the aisle. As the last of them returned to their pews, I looked out, each of them daubed with a grey star on their foreheads, and I thought then that at least Uncle Seamus was amongst his own, and offered up a prayer for him, and his friend Mr Lupelli, and all who died so far from the land of their birth.

Up in Christie's Field

The summer we camped out was a fine one. It was Mattie's idea and he had it all worked out.

"We'll get the girls to sew sacks together for a ground-sheet and there's a big bit of polythene lying in the garage we can use for a tent. A few spars from the sawmill for pegs and poles and we'll be in business."

So Mattie set his sisters to work on the sacks and we went off with the big sheet of polythene down to the stream. We floated it into the water, one transparency covering another, and followed as it drifted downriver towards the village.

"What are you at, boys?"

Jimmy Handley walked toward us on the bridge, curious about what we were up to.

"Top Secret," said Mattie, his eyes squinting in the sunlight as the polythene, the ripples and the waves of it, shimmered away from us.

"Please yourselves, lads," said Jimmy and walked off in the direction of Maggie's Bar, his cap over one eye, his dark suit shining in the light of late afternoon.

"Come on," said Mattie. "Let's go get her."

"Your fifty – and raise you fifty."

Mattie casually tossed the bill into the pot and squinted at Fergus McDermott. The bright sunshine blazed through the clear walls of our tent into his flinty grey eyes. You'd think the place was full of smoke, blinding him for a moment, that we were all in the back room of some speakeasy in Chicago, that Al Capone would be crouching down at the flaps of the tent any minute now to say, "What's new?" and give us all the password.

But I knew well what Mattie was up to. If you couldn't see his eyes you couldn't tell if he was bluffing or not. The pot, all of it cash from the McDermott's Monopoly set, stood at about £5000. The last of everyone's dough was there, and Mattie looked like he was about to cash in his chips and claim the Ballydawn Five Card Stud Championship. But it wasn't going to be that easy. I'd been watching the fall of the cards, and I reckoned I had the beating of him.

"I'm out," said Fergus, throwing in his hand.

Rory folded too.

It was my turn.

"Your fifty – and raise you five hundred."

Mattie's squint never flickered.

"OK, John Kevin. Let's see you."

He threw a pink five hundred pound note down on top of mine, and if anything squinted even more. I was starting to worry he might squeeze the eyeballs out of him the way he was going.

"Full house, Kings and Aces," I declared, showing my hand.

By now the sun was directly overhead. It was glaring through the walls of the tent, magnified by the polythene, and its heat was intense. I noticed beads of condensation starting to gather on its clear eaves, as if it was sweating on Mattie showing us his hand.

"Straight," he said calmly. "Ten, Jack, Queen, King, Ace."

He turned each card over, like Steve McQueen in The Cincinatti Kid.

"Right boys – game over," said Rory. "Let's hear it for the Ballydawn Five Card Stud Champion. Boys I give you – Matthew Murphy!"

The condensation was the first to salute him. Like liquid tickertape it started falling from the transparent walls of the tent raining down on us in great warm, wet splashes. As it hit the pot of Monopoly money, the cards, and us, it sounded like soft applause.

"Do you think there are men on other planets?" asked Fergus.

We were all settled down for the night. Each of us lay under a thick woollen blanket, our hands under our heads. Outside the last red embers of the fire were still glowing and you could feel the heat from them as the night gathered round us, close and dark and colder as the fire gradually faded.

"Don't be daft," said Mattie. "They wouldn't last five minutes – a man from Mars would be destroyed in this weather."

"But supposing he had equipment, like a suit with a special helmet, with all sorts of pipes coming out of it, or a breathing mask with a safety tube? Couldn't he survive then, Mattie?"

"Sure it would all overheat, you eejit. He'd be choking before he got any further than Ballynacray. Little green men, Fergus – why would they bother with us?"

"Perhaps they're Irish and want to come and say hello? Perhaps they're Kerrymen who landed on Mars years ago and now can't find their way home?"

"Leprechauns from outer space?" said Mattie. "Kerrymen from Mars? I think you've been reading too many comics and getting your Ireland's Own mixed up with your Superman. That's the last thing we need. Now say your prayers and go to sleep."

"Make me a blackie sossie, I want a blackie sossie, make mine black, Mattie."

Mattie crouched over the fire, a frying pan full of sausages in his hand, and worked away at the sizzling lumps of meat with a fork.

"Here, Fergus," he said. "Burnt as black as coal for you. Now John Kevin, pass me up the two there out of the wrapper."

The packet of sausages lay glistening on the dewy grass. Mattie had the fire going, sparks flying upward, the sticks glowing and hissing in the cool of dawn. I gave him two more sausages, cold and pink and plump. He fixed them onto his fork and started cooking them in the fire.

"Not too burnt for me, Mattie," I said.

He smiled and worked away. As he cooked the sausages I looked up at the sky. A great red sun loomed high above, casting a golden glow down on the hillside. Behind us stood the tent, and as we sat around in the clear light of dawn, a stillness fell on the scene.

"Is your brother coming up this afternoon, Fergus?" asked Mattie at last.

"He is surely," said Fergus. "He said he might bring us up some stuff from JonJo's."

"We could do with some more grub, right enough," said Mattie. "Make sure he brings us some sossies. These ones are going fast. And we'll get on home soon, John Kevin, and pick up some rations ourselves."

"What about more bread?" I said. "Then we could make hot dogs."

"I'll see what I can do," said Fergus. "Just as long as you'll do the sossies black, Mattie."

Mattie turned over my sausage and I watched it bronze in the red light of dawn.

"Are you sure there aren't little green men on other planets?" asked Fergus. "I swore I just saw something moving about in the sky."

"That was probably an Irish air force jet tracking down a Leprechaun flying saucer," said Mattie. "You know boys, there could be a film in this: 'Invasion of the Little Green Kerrymen'."

We both started laughing as Fergus ate up his black sausage in silence.

Mattie and I walked over the bridge towards home. The sun had risen high in the sky now and there were a few cars on the road, off to Town or perhaps going over the border. I put my hand in the pocket of my shorts.

"Here," Mattie I said. "For today."

I pulled out a thick roll of brown £100 notes. I'd nipped into the tent and taken them when everyone was eating their sossies and admiring the dawn. They would come in handy. For Rory McDermott had said he was bringing up a card school with him that afternoon, some hard chaws from Scottsville. But we'd be able for them. Today we would really clean up.

Mattie smiled. There was nothing to stop us now. Not even Little Green Kerrymen from Outer Space. They'd have to be cute to catch us.

Onion Scalp

Hegarty's dog had to be put down," said my uncle. "He loved that dog. Damn near broke his heart."

We were all going into Town, my uncle, my mother, and me. It was a bit odd to hear them talking – I felt like they'd forgotten I was in the back of the car, that I didn't really count.

"What was wrong with her?" asked my mother.

"Ach, old age as much as anything," said my uncle. "Sure the creature was blind and lame."

The car rolled on as overhead a line of tall trees dappled the light falling on the road.

"Was it Clery put her down?"

"It was. He told me in Jimmy's that he spends more time slaughtering animals than he does saving any. Says instead of being a vet he should be a butcher."

"There wouldn't be much meat on Hegarty's dog," said my mother.

"No," said my uncle. "It wouldn't amount to a decent chop."

They both fell silent as we emerged from the shade of the tall trees. I thought that they were being hard on Hegarty, whoever he was, that it would be easy to get sentimental about a dog. I imagined him as an old widower who lived on a windswept plot of land out in the wilds somewhere with hardly any company. I'd get soft about an animal if I was in his shoes.

"Is he still up in the Mental?" asked my mother at last.

"He is," said my uncle. "I can't see him leaving it. Sure there's no one for him now that the dog is gone."

I felt like crying out. Why did Hegarty have no one? Why couldn't he get another dog? Why couldn't he come out of the Mental? And what was the Mental? It sounded grim.

But I felt it wasn't my place to cry out. Besides, what could I do? I couldn't save Hegarty. I didn't even know him. I felt then like I really was invisible, that neither my uncle nor my mother could see me. But instead of this being fun, like it would be if I was a superhero, or a character in a story, I felt like a ghost, as if I'd left this life and was somewhere between here and Heaven.

"So what about Mick?" asked my uncle at last. "Any news?"

"Divil the bit," said my mother. "As long as his head hasn't expanded in this heat he should be OK."

My uncle laughed.

"He must have the quare collection of caps now," he said.

"Ten," said my mother. "One for every year we've been over. Why I have to get them for him I don't know. But it's handy we have the same sized heads – if a cap doesn't fit me it won't fit him."

"With brains that size you must be as clever as sin," said my uncle.

"Sure I'm too clever to sin," said my mother.

And then we arrived at the Diamond.

"You're back again?"

The shop assistant seemed to know my mother. He greeted her warmly, as if she had come to buy up all the caps he had. He was a thin man, tall, in a sports jacket and black slacks, and his shop smelled of must.

"I never come anywhere else," said my mother. "Sure where else would I go?"

The man smiled.

"And is it a cap you're after?"

"It is," said my mother. "Donegal Tweed if you have it."

"We have surely," said the man. "Now if you'll just come this way I can show you a lovely line in caps."

We all followed him to the far end of the shop. There was a

display cabinet there and behind the glass was a selection of grey and black speckled caps. I thought of my father, of him coming in from work in his blue boiler suit, his cap on one side, a bar of chocolate for me in his pocket.

"And I suppose you're the same size as ever?" asked the man, smiling.

"I'll have to try one on to I see," said my mother. "What about that one there?"

The man nodded and selected a key on a chain attached to his belt loop. He put the key in the panel under the glass of the cabinet, gave it a turn, and lifted the glass. The caps sat there, and I wondered whose heads they would go on, farmers, perhaps, or creamery men, or maybe garage mechanics. And if the man who owned the shop ever sold any that ended up in America.

John Wayne wore a big cap in *The Quiet Man*, but nobody in the States wore a cap these days. Cowboys wore stetsons but this shop wouldn't be selling any of those. Did the man get Yanks in his shop, anyway? You'd never know. My mother said America was full of Irish people, that half the population had Irish blood, but I thought she was exaggerating. If America was so Irish why didn't they play Gaelic football? And hurling?

"That'll do fine," said my mother. She had one of the grey and black speckled caps on her head, the peak off to one side just as my father wore his. For a moment it was a bit like seeing him.

"And I want a new hat," said my uncle. "This one's getting a bit worn."

"Certainly," said the man. "Is it a homburg you're after?"

"Yes," said my uncle. "We Murphys don't change much."

I followed them all down to the front of the shop. The man lifted the counter and went behind it.

"Now," he said to my mother, and charged her for the cap. He wrapped it in brown paper, and handed it over. "And for you, Mr Murphy, what about something like this?"

He turned round and reached up to the set of wooden shelves behind him. They were full of hats. He brought one down that was just like the one my uncle was wearing, except newer. My uncle tried it on, and walked over to a full-length mirror towards the door. We followed and the man came out from behind the counter.

"What do you think?" asked my uncle, turning to us.

"Sure it'll do fine," said my mother.

"At least it's not an oul' cap," said my uncle. I think he was cross that my mother hadn't made more of a fuss of him and his new hat.

"There's nothing oul' about this one," said my mother. Her cheeks were colouring and I knew then she was going to have a row.

"Now if you'd like to come this way –" said the man, who must have sensed what was coming. But it was too late.

"Keep out this, you!" snarled my uncle. "Now look here, Mary, I've brought you and your pup into Town to get that husband of yours his workingman's cap. You could at least be civil to me, or is this the way living with an oul' Kerry pogue has you?"

"Don't you start about Mick. It's me that's married to him, not you! If you don't like him that's your affair. But you can keep your opinions to yourself. You and your fancy homburg! You think you're a cut above the rest of us because you swan around in that post van, acting as if you own the county. Well, I knew you when you had to walk to school in your bare feet, and bawled for your supper while it was me made it for you!"

"Please, please –" said the man but it was no good. They were at each other now, and nothing was going to stop them.

"If you're as bad a cook now as you were then it's a wonder you haven't all belonging to you starved," said my uncle.

I had never seen them row before. It was all a bit of a mystery to me. I thought it must have something to do with being brother and sister. I sidled round behind my mother and hoped they would both see sense.

"I must ask you now to leave," said the man.

For a moment they both stopped and turned to him.

"Don't worry," said my mother. "We're going."

She stomped off towards the door of the shop, me trailing behind her. When she got out into the bright glare of the street she turned and waited for my uncle.

"You're nothing but an oul' Onion Scalp!' she roared as he came out behind her, in plain view of people passing us by on the pavement. "At least Mick has hair on his head, which is more than I can say for you, you fat, baldy bastard!"

It was my uncle's turn now to stomp off. I watched him get to his car, open the door, and drive off.

"The blackguard!" said my mother. We watched the car disappear and I wondered how we were going to get back.

We must have been about halfway to Ballydawn when I started to cry.

My mother had never turned round once. She marched down the road at the double, as angry as I'd ever seen her. I don't why I started crying. Fear of what lay ahead, perhaps. Upset at the row. Or maybe it was that she still hadn't acknowledged me. We must have covered nearly a couple of miles, me trailing about five paces behind her.

I thought it best to fall behind a little more. I didn't want her hearing my sniffles. It was bad enough that she was cross with Uncle Tommy; if she got cross with me as well it would be unbearable.

We came at last to Ballydawn. Still she marched on, the rage radiating out of her like it was some kind of superpower. I honestly thought she might set fire to something the way she was going, to the hedges, or the grass in the ditch, or even the very air all around her. She had turned into a ball of pure rage.

As she opened the gate I caught up and ducked in before it could swing shut again. She crunched down the gravel drive and round to the back of the house. All was quiet.

I wondered then if Uncle Tommy was lying in wait for us, if he had a shovel he would use to hit my mother over the head. I wouldn't have blamed him. Why wouldn't she turn round and see how I was?

She lifted the latch on the back door and went in. I tiptoed in behind her, scared of what might be waiting for us. There was no one in the little kitchen, so I followed her into the front room.

She was at the table, looking down at something. As I came

alongside my mother I saw what she was looking at.

There was a plate, a knife and fork either side of it, and covering the plate, Uncle Tommy's old hat, the homburg. It was then she looked at me. Her face was contorted in a strange expression, part anger still, but also part curiosity.

She lifted up Uncle Tommy's hat.

There on the plate were two big onions. There was a note as well, on a piece of paper torn from one of my cousins' jotters.

'From Onion Scalp.'

My mother looked at me.

I looked at my mother.

And suddenly we both burst out laughing.

The Smugglers

I looked out of the window as the little hills rolled past, a blaze of sunshine on them, the grey road unwinding before us. The car lurched up and down and I could feel my stomach leap, a giddy thrill running through me. It was like being on a rollercoaster, see-sawing along at 50mph, flying through the air in Uncle Tommy's Morris Minor, on our way to the Border.

"Much news of Mrs Reilly?"

My mother, sat behind my aunt and uncle with me and my cousins Matt and Mary, addressed her question to the back of Auntie Lizzie's head. Auntie Lizzie was wearing a glorious hat, done like a turban with a pattern of large red roses printed on the brown fabric. I could see her face in Uncle Tommy's rear view mirror, the fly-away frames of her specs, her red cheeks, her brown button eyes, and thought she looked like a genie released from the lamp.

"Divil the bit. She's much the same, Mary. The daughter visits her three times a week, but I don't think she's long for this world."

"Oh dear," said my mother. "I suppose it'll be a mercy for her."

"It will of course," said Auntie Lizzie.

The Morris Minor rumbled on, careering up and down the drumlins. Outside, green fields and low grey walls passed by. Somewhere up ahead lay the Border. I'd never been to the Border before. It sounded very far away, like Checkpoint Charlie, or the dark side of the moon.

They'd fallen quiet now. Mrs Reilly was Uncle Tommy and Auntie Lizzie's next door neighbour. I remembered us calling in on her, getting an apple and a cup of milk each, her kindness, her warm heart, and then I looked out of the window, and a field of cows looked back at me, unblinking, chewing idly away.

"And what about Jackie Stone?" asked my mother.

"Jackie?" said Auntie Lizzie. "Jackie's going to England in October. Birmingham. He has a job lined up with the uncle. Ballydawn will be a lot quieter when he's gone."

Uncle Tommy pulled up at a roadside garage, a couple of pumps and a faded sign saying 'McGuigan's' blistering in the heat. He got out, walked a couple of paces over to one of the pumps, lifted off the petrol cap, and stuck the nozzle into the tank. You could hear it filling up as he squeezed the trigger, a kind of low gurgling sound, and then Uncle Tommy was getting back into the car, slamming the door, and we were off again.

"And how's Mick?" asked Auntie Lizzie.

"Ach, just the same," said my mother. "He's at home, painting the house. You'd hardly think he was Irish at all, the way he's never over." My ears pricked up at news of my father, but my mother fell silent again and the sound of the car's engine drowned out my thoughts.

We rolled on down the road for a good few miles, the sun getting warmer all the while. Uncle Tommy had said that rain was forecast but the way the sun was shining I couldn't see it. Everyone was quiet, stupefied by the heat, and I started to dream of ice creams, of sliders, and choc ices, and cones with flakes in them. I hoped we'd soon be at the Border and that my mother would get me one when we arrived.

A large grey stone church loomed up ahead, and as we passed I twisted around to see its black signboard. 'Our Lady Of Grace, Scottsville'. Everyone started blessing themselves, so I quickly blessed myself as well. I hoped no one would notice I wasn't as fast at blessing myself as the rest of them.

Nobody said a word.

Uncle Tommy drove along, the garage and church far behind,

only fields on either side of us now, out in the wilds of the county. The countryside was green and lush and lovely, and although the heat was fierce it was great to be driving along in it.

Up ahead a large black car was halted in the road, crossways. A fat man in a dark suit stood beside it, and turned when he heard us approaching.

Uncle Tommy slowed down. As we drew nearer I saw that the fat man was wearing a dog collar, and that his face was very red. The car stopped and Uncle Tommy wound down his window.

"Can I help you, Father?"

"Thank God!" said the cleric. "There's a diocesan meeting of parish priests at Our Lady of Grace's in an hour. Do you think you could get a mechanic to come out and help me? I passed a garage on the way down – if you could get word to them I'd be eternally grateful. Tell them the diocese will bear any expense."

"I will of course, your reverence."

Uncle Tommy started the ignition, and we were off again, the image of the prelate getting smaller and smaller in the rear view mirror as the car sped away.

"Who was that, Daddy?" asked Mary.

"That was the bishop," said Uncle Tommy. "And we'd better do as he asks. For all I know he has a note of the registration number – he could excommunicate us if I don't."

"What does excommunicate mean, Daddy?" asked Mary.

"It means he could stop Daddy receiving Holy Communion," said Matt.

"Oh, Daddy!" said Mary. "Hurry up!"

The grown-ups were laughing, but Uncle Tommy was driving faster now. Up ahead I could see the garage the bishop had mentioned and Uncle Tommy started slowing down. He pulled in to the forecourt and got out of the car.

He went into the shop and talked to the man behind the counter. The man was wearing a light brown coat like a greengrocer's, and seemed more interested in his newspaper than he did in Uncle Tommy. There was some pointing by my uncle, some nodding by the man, then Uncle Tommy bought a packet of Capstan and the man gave him his change. He was soon back in the car and then we were away again.

"What did he say, Tommy?" asked Auntie Lizzie as we rolled along.

"He just said he'd look into it."

There was a pause then Auntie Lizzie said, "Do you think he might be of the other persuasion?"

"That'll be the bishop stranded if he is," said Uncle Tommy.

We all fell quiet and the car trundled on for a good few miles until up ahead there was a road block and policemen waving us down.

The Border.

"Hello, Officer," said Uncle Tommy, coming alongside one of them. "Nice day."

The policeman said nothing but the barrier across the road lifted and he waved us through. We'd crossed the Border but everything looked much the same: the sun was blazing down, the fields were as green as ever, the low-lying stone walls just as grey.

"Are we in another country now?" I asked.

Uncle Tommy caught my eye in the rear-view mirror.

"Does it all look like the one country to you?" he asked.

"Yes," I said.

"Then pass no remark," he said.

He turned his eyes back to the road, and I wondered if I'd said something I shouldn't have.

Up ahead there was a signpost and the name of a town I couldn't quite catch. We were coming to the outskirts of it now, past white houses with small green gardens in front and cars parked on the kerb. Uncle Tommy went past them, round a small roundabout and then turned into a big road, with shops and pubs and a small monument down at the end it, strollers in short sleeves and summer dresses walking along the pavements in the blazing sunshine. He parked outside a supermarket and turned round to talk to us.

"Wait here," he said. "If you're good children you'll get sweets."

The grown-ups all got out and went into the supermarket. By

now the sun was high overhead, blazing down fiercely on us, and I wondered why we couldn't get out of the car.

"Do you think they'll come back with ice creams?" I said to Matt.

"You wouldn't know what they're up to," he said. "Wind down that window. If it gets any hotter in here I'll melt."

I wound down the window on my side and Mattie wound down his window. There wasn't much of a breeze but a little air blew into the hot, stuffy Morris Minor. I started to get uneasy. Ever since the Border everyone seemed to be on edge, and I thought about the policemen, the roadblock, the checkpoint.

I wondered if Uncle Tommy and Auntie Lizzie might be spies. That would explain why there were so tight-lipped about everything. I wasn't even sure why we'd actually come here. Were Uncle Tommy and Auntie Lizzie both on a secret mission, like Napoleon Solo and Illya Kuryakin in *The Man From Uncle*, fighting the forces of THRUSH? Uncle Tommy and Auntie Lizzie didn't look like secret agents – they were a bit too stout. But you could never tell. After all who would have thought that the United Network Command for Law and Enforcement had their headquarters in a tailor's shop? That was the thing about spying – you couldn't take anything at face value. I bet Uncle Tommy and Auntie Lizzie were spies, and had gadgets just like they did on TV, pens that were walkie-talkies, cigarette cases that turned into tape-recorders, lighters that took pictures. And I bet they had those shoulder holsters like they did on *The Man From Uncle* too, tucked under their armpits with their guns peeking out. Wait a minute! What about my mother? Was she in on all of this? Was she part of Uncle Tommy and Auntie Lizzie's secret spy ring?!

"Here," said my mother. "I got you a wafer."

My mother handed me a slider, and I took it from her and started licking at the drips from it, then worked my way down the cool creamy white block of ice cream.

Uncle Tommy was round at the back of the Morris Minor, and I heard him slam the boot. The grown-ups all got back into the car and he started her up. I thought Auntie Lizzie looked a bit awkward settling herself into the passenger seat, but soon the engine was growling again and we were off.

"Are you sure you got everything?" asked my mother.

Uncle Tommy looked at her in the rear view mirror.

"Nothing to declare," he said, and smiled at her, a big broad smile, and we were away.

"Have you much in the boot?"

The policeman squinted in the sunshine, bent down to talk to Uncle Tommy through his open window.

"Just a few bits and pieces, Officer," said Uncle Tommy.

"Do you mind if I have a look?"

"Not at all," said Uncle Tommy.

My heart started to thump. That supermarket – was it the HQ of Uncle Tommy's spy network? Was he working for an Irish branch of the United Network Command for Law and Enforcement? Was my uncle actually a man from UNCLE himself? Had he hidden an arsenal of secret gadgets in the boot of his Morris Minor?

The policeman walked slowly round to the back of the car. I could hear his heavy tread and the boot opening and then silence. I started to sweat. We were for it now. Then there was an almighty thump and more footsteps.

"Fine," said the policeman, coming alongside the window again. "All in order."

Uncle Tommy smiled, and as we drove off I could see the policeman looking at us in the rear view mirror as the car pulled away.

Auntie Lizzie started giggling.

"It's not the boot he needed to be looking in!" she said between gusts of laughter.

They were all laughing now, Uncle Tommy and Auntie Lizzie in stitches, my mother in tears, as Auntie Lizzie reached down the front of her enormous bosom.

"But it's all starting to melt!" she cried.

I craned over the seat to see what Auntie Lizzie was laughing at. There, in the ample folds of her cleavage, were several packs of butter, yellow and soft from the heat of the day. A wet stain was starting to spread across the front of her black dress, like a map of America, only done in butter.

"John Kevin, open that window for me, would you?"

I leaned over her, straining to reach the winder that would let down the window.

"Hurry up!" she said, giggling away. "I'm getting covered in the stuff!"

I struggled with the winder. It wasn't easy turning it, leaning over my aunt, the great bulk of her, with the car careering over the drumlins, but eventually I managed to get it going and wound the window down.

She pulled the softened packets of butter out of bosom, in hysterics now, and ditched them into the road. Then she lifted up her hat. There stood another pack of Kerrygold balanced perfectly on her black hair, the gold foil of the wrapper starting to sag in the heat.

"At least we have this one!" she cried.

Uncle Tommy nearly swerved off the road.

"Quick!" she cried, catching the pack of butter in her hands. "Put your foot down, Tommy! Before this one goes as well!"

The car suddenly lurched forward and then we were going like blazes. I leaned over to look at the speedometer – 65mph! Uncle Tommy was driving like Jackie Stewart! We bumped and rattled along, flying now over the little hills, till a familiar figure came into view up ahead.

It was the bishop, still stuck in the middle of the road.

He looked puzzled as we came racing towards him, then jumped out of the way as we flew past. I looked in the rear view mirror to see him growing smaller and smaller behind us, shaking his fist, his face crimson with anger. Was it a sin to smuggle butter across the Border? What if it all melted before you got home? Perhaps the bishop would know.

But it was too late now to stop and ask him. Soon he had disappeared altogether, and I realised that borders didn't only mark out one territory from another. They also marked out who was in your gang and who outside it, who was an outlaw and who wasn't.

I looked out of the window, the countryside different somehow from when we'd all set out, Uncle Tommy in shirt sleeves, racing home before our contraband melted clean away, a car full of fugitives out-pacing the long shadow of the law.

A Day at the Seaside

"The English are the best, the English are the best, after the Irish the English are the best!"

"Would you be quiet?" barked Uncle Tommy, glaring in the rear view mirror.

Mattie fell silent. Now we would just have to be good boys until we got to Blackrock. We were on our way to the seaside, somewhere near Dublin, and as the countryside rolled away behind us I looked out of the window of Uncle Tommy's car.

The car rolled on and the heat got worse. I could tell Mattie was itching to have another go at me, to torment me some more. But there was nothing he could do – he'd just have to be quiet all the way to Blackrock.

Eventually Uncle Tommy said, "Nearly there," and I saw a sign that read 'Blackrock 10'. I could almost feel the sea breeze on me now – I was longing to get out of the car and run down to the ocean, to dive into the cold water, to shout and bawl and yell that Mattie was the best, Mattie was the best, Mattie was an annoying little pest.

Uncle Tommy, Auntie Lizzie, and my mother laid out a few towels on the beach, and settled down to soak up the sun. Uncle Tommy had the paper, the *Irish Press*, and sat with his legs stretched out before him, his trousers rolled up below the knee. My mother and Auntie Lizzie sat down as well, their summer frocks and pastel cardigans a splash of colour against the drab brown sand. They started fanning themselves with their hands, and told us kids to go off and play.

Mattie and I wandered down to the shore, while the girls went off in the opposite direction. I waited for Mattie to start. Now that there were no grown-ups to keep us apart I expected more of his slanging.

"Shall we forget who's the best?" said Mattie.

I looked at him to see if he was trying to fool me.

"We're flesh and blood, John Kevin. Cousins. You're a part of me, and I'm a part of you."

I wasn't expecting this. Mattie stood against the sun, the sky cloudless and blue and as vast as the sea that stretched out before us.

"Blood brothers?" I said.

"Blood brothers," said Mattie. "Here."

He took a penknife from the pocket of his shorts and eased the blade out. He drew the knife across his thumb and a bright line of blood appeared in the slice. There wasn't a flicker from him as he looked steadily into my eyes. He handed the knife to me and I set about cutting my own thumb just like he had. Once the blood was drawn I held it up for Mattie to press his bloody thumb against my own.

"Brothers by blood, brothers forever," said Mattie.

"Brothers forever, brothers by blood," I answered.

Suddenly behind us we could hear footsteps running. We turned to see Auntie Lizzie and my mother flying at us.

"What are you at?" cried Auntie Lizzie.

They both gave us a clip around the ear and dragged us back to where they were sitting.

"Come here," said Auntie Lizzie.

She rooted around in her handbag and pulled out some Elastoplast and a small pair of scissors.

"You're savages, the pair of you!" my mother cried. "You'd think you had no breeding at all."

Auntie Lizzie finished placing the Elastoplast over our cuts and tugged it tight on each of our thumbs in turn.

"Now run off and play," said Auntie Lizzie. "And Mattie – give me that knife."

Mattie handed it over, and off we set again for the shore.

As we got to the water's edge I thought I saw something glinting in the sun. I bent down and there was a Coke bottle, the metal cap still on the top of it, spots of rust round the rim. I got a shock when I saw the piece of paper inside.

"Hey, Mattie!" I called. "Come and have a look at this!"

He was paddling in the shallows just up the beach from where I was, shoes and socks on the sand, splashing away, raising up a froth of water as he jigged and kicked in the sea.

"What is it?" he called.

"It's a message in a bottle!"

He came then, curiosity on every inch of his face.

"Would you look at that?" he said, squinting through the glass as I held up the bottle. "Come on, John Kevin, let's get the lid off and see what it says."

He grabbed the bottle from me and wrenched at the cap with his finger and thumb. He up-ended the bottle and the small packet of paper, folded up into a tight little square, dropped out onto the sand. I bent down quickly and picked it up.

It was a half a page torn from a jotter, a scrawled note covering a few of the thin blue lines, the pencilled letters faded and grey.

I read the words slowly, quietly.

"By the time you get this I'll probably be dead. Our ship is being attacked by the Japs. Tell my brother – ".

The message broke off after 'brother'.

Mattie and I looked at each other, eyes wide.

"This bottle…" said Mattie quietly. "Whoever threw it into the sea hoped someone would find it. That someone is you. But we'll never know who wrote the message. Looks like they didn't get time to say who they were. But why the brother? Why not their mother or father, their sweetheart, their best friend?"

I looked out to sea. Somewhere beyond the horizon a ship lay at the bottom of the ocean.

Mattie's questions hung in the air.

"Those brothers must have been close," said Mattie. "As close as blood brothers."

A shiver ran through me then, and I thought who would I want to call out to if I knew I was about to die.

"Say nothing of this, John Kevin. This must be our secret. There's no way we can ever find out who threw this bottle into the ocean, no way we can find the brother. All we can do is say a prayer, and hope that they're in heaven."

Mattie took the page from me and folded up the paper. He put it back in the bottle and banged the cap into place. Then he floated the bottle out to sea and we looked after it as the waves carried it off the way it had come. Glints from the sun caught in the bottle's glass for a while and then were gone, like a signal fading and slowly dying.

We turned and walked back towards Uncle Tommy, Auntie Lizzie, and my mother. The girls had joined them and they were all eating sandwiches, passing round a bottle of cream soda, smiling and looking pleased with themselves in the sun.

"Well," said Uncle Tommy as we came up to them. "Any mermaids down by the shore?" He laughed at us, at the confused look on our faces.

We sat down, not speaking, looking out to the horizon. The sun was declining now and the day cooling, the breeze fresher.

"Brothers by blood, brother forever," I murmured quietly

"Brothers forever, brother by blood," Mattie replied, just as softly.

We watched the sun dip down, the blue sky turning red and purple. I wondered if Mattie's thumb throbbed like mine, if he had the same ache as me.

Later we travelled back to Ballydawn, the night soon upon us, black and cold, and for the first time since I was small I grew afraid of the dark.

On the Cards

A re you robbing, Evelyn?"

We sat round the table in my aunt and uncle's front room, each of us holding our cards. My mother had dealt them, threes and twos, turning one up on the deck by way of trumps when she'd finished giving them all out. It was the Jack of Clubs, a steal for anyone holding the Ace.

"I am, Auntie Mary," said Evelyn. She lifted the Jack, settled it in her hand, and put the one down on top of the deck. Twenty-five was a curious game, somewhere between Poker and Whist. You could play it with partners, and there were trumps, and it seemed especially Irish.

It was fast and easy once you got the hang of it, three parts luck to one part skill, just about the right ratio for a good card game. My cousins Geraldine, Evelyn, and Anna were playing with my mother and me. Everyone else was away up to Town. Johnny was starting at the Tech in the autumn and needed new duds. So they'd all gone off to get him a new rig-out.

"Now the sport begins," said my mother. I reckoned she thought she was a dab hand at Twenty-five, that she could beat the rest of us by a mixture of codology, luck, and the bit of skill the game called for. But I knew from practice that anyone could win given the right hand.

The cards fell as we all played our opening gambits. My cousin Geraldine led the King of Diamonds, then Anna played the Three, and I played the Ten. I didn't have much of a hand, in fact I had a hand like a fist, but I thought I could get at least one trick this go-round. Evelyn played the Ace of Clubs and it was now my mother's turn. It looked like Evelyn had the trick – her trump would take it.

"You thought you had that one, Evelyn," said my mother. "But how's that for a crafty move?"

My mother threw down the Ace of Hearts. The trick was hers!

She went on to take the next two, leading with the King of Spades and then the Three. Now it was down to Evelyn to make her play – she still had the Jack of Trumps, the second highest card in the deck. Again we went round. My mother led with the King of Hearts, Geraldine played the Seven, Anna the Ten. It was time to make my move. I threw down the Three of Clubs. All our eyes were on Evelyn. What was she going to play?

Evelyn laid the Jack with a big hearty laugh and the initiative was back with her. She took the tricks and threw down her next card as if she was throwing down a gauntlet.

"Now, Auntie Mary, what do you think of that?"

Evelyn had laid the Five of Trump, the Fingers, and the trick was hers. Nothing could beat the Fingers and I winced a little inside as she took the cards. Looked like this game was a straight fight between my mother and Evelyn. Perhaps I would have better luck in the next hand.

The back door opened and we heard footsteps in the kitchen.

"Hello? Anyone at home?"

A rather tall figure in a long brown dress and green Crimplene cardigan, with dark hair done in a bun and round hornrimmed spectacles stood in front of us by the door.

"Hello, Mary," said the woman.

It was Mrs Ford. She lived up the road in Ballydawn, and was much older than my mother, and quite wiry. My mother told me she had knitting needle elbows, that when my mother was a girl Mrs Ford used to get her to do messages for her, and was always giving her a dig with them.

"Hello, Mrs Ford," said my mother. "We were just playing a few hands of Twenty-five. Do you fancy a game?"

"I don't mind if I do," said Mrs Ford, and came and sat alongside me, peering over the rims of her specs at us all. I was a bit wary of her. I didn't want Mrs Ford elbowing me with those pointy elbows of hers. As my mother was always saying didn't I bruise easier than fruit?

We played out our game. My mother took five tricks first, and so she got to Twenty-five and won. Then we played a few more hands, Mrs Ford included now, doing as well as my mother had done, till in the end the scores stood at three games each to them, with Geraldine taking one game, and me the other.

"Now, Mary," said Mrs Ford, addressing my mother. "Would you ever read my fortune?"

My ears pricked up like a donkey's. I'd never heard of my mother telling fortunes before. I thought it was something only gypsies did, and wasn't something a good Catholic should indulge in. But straight away my mother's face lit up. I got the feeling she liked having an audience, of being the centre of attention.

She gathered up all the cards and shuffled them. Then she handed them to Mrs Ford and asked her to lay out seven cards face down on the table. This looked a bit like Patience to me but I said nothing. I was becoming absorbed in the ritual, in the look of concentration on my mother's face and the atmosphere of the forbidden that was growing round the table.

Mrs Ford laid out the cards just as my mother had told her. Then my mother asked her to turn up the first card. Mrs Ford laid down the deck and turned up the card. It was the King of Diamonds.

"In this column," said my mother, "the cards will tell your fortune in terms of Wealth. The King of Diamonds is a very powerful card. He represents a rich man, or a large windfall, or money coming to you from the government. So far so good. Now, turn up the next card, Mrs Ford." She turned the card over to reveal the King of Clubs.

"In this column come cards to do with Health. The King of Clubs denotes some sorrow or setback in terms of your health. Have you been ill lately Mrs Ford?"

"No, not at all, Mary. Just the same as ever."

"Well the next column is all about Love, so why don't we see what the cards say they have in store for you here?"

Mrs Ford looked a bit of unsure of herself now, I thought, but she turned up a card in the third column.

"The Two of Clubs," said my mother. "Now Clubs again represents sorrow or setbacks, but as this is only a low card all that's indicated is perhaps a tiff with Mr Ford, or some kind of falling out you make up quickly enough for it not to be the end of the world. Now what about the next one? The cards in this column are all about Family."

Mrs Ford turned over the card in the fourth column.

The Ace of Spades.

My mother mother went white.

"Well, Mary?" said Mrs Ford. "What does the card say?"

I watched my mother's face closely. She was very quiet, the previous mood of parlour games and naughtiness gone now.

"The Ace of Spades," said my mother. "It's a... sad card. It signals the end of something."

"Like what?" said Mrs Ford sharply. I got the impression that this wasn't the kind of fortune telling she had in mind when she suggested my mother read the cards.

"All of the cards tell a story, your future revealed in each one. But I have to see them to get the whole story. Why not turn up the next one?"

By now my cousins weren't smiling like they had at the start of all this. Anna started fidgeting and Evelyn had to give her a poke with her elbow. As Mrs Ford was turning up the next card my mother gave them both a sharp look.

"Now," said Mrs Ford. "The Ten of Hearts. What do you make of that Mary?"

"This column is all about friends. So expect a gathering, a party or a wedding or a —"

"Wake?" said Anna.

Everyone turned to look at her.

"Don't be daft," said Evelyn. "Sure you were never at a wake in your life."

"I was so. Wasn't I at Auntie Annie's? Do you not remember Auntie Mary coming over?"

"Wisht!" cried Evelyn.

"Could she be right, Mary?" asked Mrs Ford. Her face now had a worried look, as if what had started out as a bit of fun had turned into something more disturbing.

"Not at all," said my mother. "Like I said Mrs Ford it's how the other cards fall and the way they line up against each other. Shall we have a look at the next one?"

Mrs Ford looked doubtful, afraid even. But like a sleepwalker who has no control over what they were doing she reached over and turned up the next card.

"The Queen of Clubs," said my mother, assuming command of the situation. "This is about the Future."

"Oh my God!" said Mrs Ford. "There's a whole heap of sorrow coming my way!"

She got up and ran from the table, through the kitchen, and out the back door. My mother looked stunned. Anna reached over and turned up the last card. It was the Jack of Hearts.

"What does it mean, Auntie Mary? What's this card all about?" cried Anna.

"That's enough fun for one day," said my mother. She gathered up the cards and told us all to go out and play. We all looked at one another but did as she said. Whatever she'd seen in the cards the rest of us couldn't fathom.

What did it all mean?

The news came later that night.

Mr Ford had suffered a stroke, and was up in the hospital. I asked my mother if this was what she had seen in the cards.

"There's worse to come," was all she would say.

When he died a week later I thought that was the end of it. We would be going back to London on Saturday. It seemed as if my mother couldn't wait to get out of Ballydawn.

We stood on the road outside my aunt and uncle's house, my mother's big black holdall at our feet.

Everyone had come to see us off. It had been a brilliant summer, one of the best. But I couldn't help thinking about poor Mrs Ford. My mother wouldn't say any more about the afternoon she read her fortune. All she'd say was that a pack of cards was the Devil's work.

I thought about all of this as the taxi pulled up.

"Off to Monaghan?" said the driver, winding down his window.

"We are," said my mother. "Come on, John, Let's go."

We said our goodbyes, and promised to write a few lines once we were back. And then we were in the car and away. I watched my aunt and uncle and all of my cousins grow smaller in the rear view mirror. I was so intent on watching them I hadn't paid proper attention to what the driver and my mother were saying.

"Aye, last night," said the driver. "The same as her husband. You've never seen anything like it. She just keeled over."

It took me a while to work out what they were saying.

It was Mrs Ford. She'd collapsed at her husband's wake and died in the same hospital.

My mother never read fortunes again.

The Curate

Do you know how babies are made?" whispered Mattie.
We were all just on our way in to Mass so the question surprised me.

"Something to do with – you know…" I whispered back.

We arrived at the door of the church. There was a good crowd inside, all in their Sunday Best, walking down the aisles to find a seat. We blessed ourselves with holy water from the font in the porch and followed Uncle Tommy, Auntie Lizzie, and my mother to a pew about halfway down, and all squeezed past each other to kneel on the hard runner and say our prayers.

I never really understood why we were all up and down so much at Mass, why we couldn't just sit on the pew and say our prayers like that. Perhaps I was just a lazy pup, as Mr O'Reilly called me once after we'd had a school Mass in London. He'd seen me kneeling with my bum shoved up against the pew, but it wasn't laziness that made me do that – it was a terrible tiredness that always seemed to come over me whenever I heard the drone of prayers and breathed in the aroma of incense. I'd go into a drowse, and that morning was particularly bad.

I'd had no breakfast and between the hunger, the prayers, the swinging ciborium, and the early start I must have forgotten myself. I'd seen Timothy Desmond stick his bum into the pew in front of me and it looked a very comfortable way to get through the big kneeling part of Mass towards the end. But Mr O'Reilly had no sympathy. He slippered my bum and said it would serve to remind me that bums should be kept out of sight in the House of God.

As a mark of respect.

I was thinking all of this when Mattie hissed at me.

"Well," he whispered. "What about babies?"

Before I could reply a bell tinkled and the priest came out of a side door by the altar with his altar servers. The whole church stood and Mass began.

I wasn't feeling so good that morning. I had a bit of a cold, a summer cold my mother called it, and I wished I'd been able to stay at my aunt and uncle's house instead of having to go to Mass. But no one missed Mass in Ireland. I couldn't even miss one Sunday when I wasn't feeling great. But it wasn't the cold that concerned me so much now.

For I couldn't stop thinking about Mattie's question. How are babies made? It was hard to know for sure. I'd heard all sorts of rumours. Colin Woodcock said babies were made by mummies rubbing a special cream produced by daddies into their bosoms. Nine months later babies came out of the crack in the mummy's cleavage. But Tony de Silva said that that wasn't how babies were made, that Colin Woodcock had got it all wrong. He said that the daddy had to lie on top of the mummy and whisper a secret word that only mummies and daddies knew into the mummy's ear. Jack Dutton said that couldn't be right, that some mummies were deaf and they still had babies so how could a daddy make a baby with a mummy who couldn't hear the special secret word? He said babies were made by the priest giving a blessing to mummies and daddies and then God let them have a baby if they'd been good. Simon Goddard said that sounded too much like Santa bringing you toys for Christmas. He said it was to do with the birds and the bees but we all reckoned that was completely daft. So Mattie's question had me stumped. How are babies made?

"In the name of the Father, and of the Son, and of the Holy Ghost."

"Amen."

We all sat on the hard pews.

Up until this point I'd been going through the motions, up and down like a sleepwalker as the drone of the prayers and the heavy scent of incense from the previous Mass still hung in the dusty air of the church. There must have been about four hundred people there at least. And now all our eyes were on the young curate. At last I started to wake up a bit.

I'd heard he was new, a young freshly ordained priest from Leitrim. This was his first parish and now here he was, giving his first sermon. I took out my hankie and blew my nose. I didn't want to be honking into it while he was speaking.

"My brothers and sisters," he said, "we are all children of God. Today's Gospel is all about Our Lord's attitude to children. First He heals a stricken child. Then He sets a little one amidst His disciples, and says that whoever receives a child in the name of Our Lord receives Him; and whoever receives Our Lord receives the One who sent Him. Then He says that whoever scandalizes a child it were better for him that a millstone were hanged around his neck, and he were cast into the sea. Now here we have the two ends of faith: that those who receive the Word of the Lord in humility and simplicity like a child will know the Father and His infinite love and mercy. But those who reject the teachings of faith, who in particular scandalize a child, it were better for him that a millstone were hanged around his neck and he were cast in the sea. Now what does it to mean, to scandalize? Well, my brothers and sisters, we all know scandal. Along with gossip and the spreading of rumours scandal is a giving in to worldliness, to the vices those who ignore the Gospel recklessly indulge in."

I noticed that the curate had very red hair, ginger in fact. He was like Terry O'Gorman, a friend of Mattie's who was always up to mischief. I wondered if mischief was as bad as scandal, if mischief was a child's version of giving in to worldliness. What did Our Lord make of Terry O'Gorman, I wondered.

"Brothers and sisters," he said, "in our workaday world where bills have to be paid, where jobs have to be done, where children have to be reared and the elderly looked after, it is easy to lose sight of today's Gospel. It is easy to become dulled and hardened by the demands of the world. It is easy for us to become lax about our faith. But in the week ahead I ask that we all think about the words of today's Gospel, that we try to retain the simplicity, the innocence, the innate kindness and loveability of children. For of such is the Kingdom of God. In the name of the Father, and of the Son, and of the Holy Ghost."

We all stood for the Creed, all said the prayer together. With the Gospel and the priest's sermon over, Mass was moving towards Holy Communion. I brought out my hankie again and blew my nose and tried to think holy thoughts and say holy prayers.

Soon the priest was elevating the Host and we were kneeling again. It was a sacred moment, this. An altar server rang the bell and we all bowed our heads, beating our breasts and saying very quietly, "Jesus, my Lord and my God," worshipping our Maker held aloft in the priest's freckled white hands. He came down to the altar rails and slowly everyone started to go up to receive Holy Communion.

I was in the procession advancing towards the priest now, my head bowed, my hands joined. I was worried my nose was going to run, that I would need my hankie just as I got to the altar rails, that my summer cold would show me up in some way. But you couldn't pull out of the procession once you'd started going forwards. That would be even more of an embarrassment. How would you ever get back to your seat? What would people think? Would the priest see you and say something? That would be terrible!

We shuffled forwards and I arrived at the head of the communicants, just in front of the priest. He looked me straight in the eyes and a terrible feeling came over me. A sneeze was building in my nose. But I couldn't stop now. He was about to give me the Host. As I opened my mouth, stuck out my tongue, and closed my eyes I suddenly let out a great A-CHOO!

I opened my eyes to see an appalling sight.

There on the gold brocade of the priest's vestments was a lace of spray from me all over his chest. He must have managed to pull away the sacred Host only just in time. Our eyes met again.

Without saying another word I turned quickly and walked back to where I'd been sitting.

"Well, John Kevin," whispered Mattie in the back of my uncle's Morris Minor. "What about babies?"

I looked out of the window. It was very uncomfortable in the back of the car. It had been built to hold five, two in the front and three in the back, but there were actually four of us in the back and it was a very tight squeeze. So this was one reason why I didn't want to be bothered with Mattie's question.

But beyond him was the anguish I felt about sneezing instead of receiving. It was such a terrible thing to happen. No one had said anything about it but I knew that eventually they would all know. I might have been the last one of us up to receive but word would get round. And then what would they say? That it was typical of the Godless English, that what a kind of a boy was I at all, that I should be ashamed and so should all belonging to me.

"What did you think of Fr O'Rourke, Tommy?"

My mother, squeezed tight in beside Mattie, addressed her question to the back of my uncle's head.

"He's a bit young," said Uncle Tommy. "But then I suppose if he's had the call, fair play to him."

"Sure it's a lonely life for any man, being a priest," said my aunt.

"Good luck to him," said my uncle. "But by the time you're ready to be a priest you must know what you're letting yourself in for."

"Pass no remark," said my mother. "The Church may be changing but the Faith stays the same."

"Babies!" hissed Mattie, as the grown-ups went on talking. "Where do they come from?"

I turned to look at him. It was happening again. I couldn't get at my hankie – we were all too squashed in together.

I sneezed all over him.

"Come on, John Kevin," said Mattie. "Let's get out on the bikes."

We had changed out of our good clothes into shorts and shirts and snakebelts and we'd had our dinner. A summer cold was a funny thing. Although I'd been struck down I didn't feel too bad, not like I did with a winter cold. Perhaps it was the warm weather.

It was hot outside as we hopped on the bikes. It was great to be out and away, riding off to wherever Mattie was heading, the sun high overhead, a Sunday hush over the countryside, hardly a car on the road.

Mattie slowed down and came alongside me.

"Well," he said. "Do you want me to tell you how babies are made?"

"OK," I said. Perhaps he knew something I didn't.

"The daddy puts his mickey into the mammy," he said. "The daddy puts a special seed in the mammy's belly and nine months later when the baby is grown from the seed out it pops."

I nearly fell off the bike.

This was different from anything else I'd heard. No cream, no special word, no blessing. But I didn't quite understand.

"And what part of the mummy does the daddy put his willy in?" I asked.

"He puts it into her hole," said Mattie.

Now I was really mystified. Did mummies have holes? Where?

"What hole?" I asked.

Mattie laughed.

"Did you never see a bull up at a cow? The bull puts his big pizzle into the cow's hole. It's just like that with the daddy and the mammy."

"No," I said, "I've never been that close to either a bull or a cow. Are you telling me that mummies have holes specially made for daddies to put their willies in?"

Now Mattie nearly fell off his bike. He was laughing so much he'd started to wobble on the sit-up-and-beg. In the end he dismounted and stood holding it by the handlebars at the side of the road. I got off mine and came alongside him.

"You don't know much, do you, John Kevin?" he said, grinning all over his face.

I thought about it for a bit.

Mattie probably had it all wrong like the rest of them. What he said made about as much sense as any other story I'd heard.

"There aren't a lot of bulls and cows in London," I said.

"Well – now you know. And when the daddy puts his mickey into the mammy that's called 'sex' ".

"What about when the bull puts his pizzle into the cow?"

"That's sex too," said Mattie. "Come on," he said, hopping back up on the bike. "Let's get out to the woods and do some tracking."

I crawled forward on my stomach. Mattie was up ahead, on his stomach too, wriggling through the trees as if he was Davy Crockett. A canopy of leaves overhead mottled the sunlight and made the woods more gloomy than the sunny countryside round about. I imagined we were on the trail of the Apaches, that this was the Wild West, that up ahead lay their wigwams.

But the problem was the ground. It was full of twigs and mushed up leaves and dirt, and crawling along on it was very uncomfortable. In fact, it was painful. My bare legs were scratched and I was sure my knees were bleeding. I wished Mattie would stop, but he carried on wriggling like a snake through the undergrowth.

We were now deep into the forest. I wasn't sure how long we'd been tracking, but it felt like half an hour. I was getting tired of the whole thing. If this was Mattie's idea of fun he could count me out. Suddenly he stopped. He held his hand up for me to stop too, and half turned his head. He put his finger to his lips to signal that I should be quiet.

It was then that I heard the noises.

"Ooh, ooh, ooh!"

I couldn't make out what it was. It sounded at first like a bird, trapped in the branches of a tree perhaps, but then I realised it wasn't a bird at all. It was the voice of a girl, and she sounded like she was being attacked.

I edged forward as quietly as I could. Through a gap in the trees up ahead I saw what was making the noises.

Fr O'Rourke was in front of Terence O'Gorman's sister. He seemed to be buffeting her, to be rubbing up against her with his belly. His trousers were down around his ankles and his white bottom rose and fell as he buffeted. She had her eyes closed and was making the noises.

Three things then happened all at once: I sneezed. Terence O'Gorman's sister let a long low moan out of her. Mattie turned round, a horrified look on his face.

He got up quickly and started running. I got up and stumbled after him.

I heard Fr O'Rourke calling after us, "Who's there?" but by then I was running, running as fast I could, until I had followed Mattie out of the woods, onto the bikes and away, the image of what I'd seen playing over and over in my mind.

Up ahead Mattie was flying along on his bike. I pedalled after him with all that I was made of, and eventually drew level. Mattie was laughing his head off.

"Well, John Kevin," he said between guffaws. "Do you believe me now?"

I dropped back behind him, and took a look over my shoulder. Did Fr O'Rourke have a car? Supposing he caught up with us? What would he say? I tried to catch Mattie up again, and thought then that he was right, that I didn't know very much, that even though I was going up to big school after the holidays I was still a child.

And I rode as hard as I could away from the dark wood.

Picking Up Sticks

McClintock's Lane lay at the back of my aunt and uncle's house, away down the field and to the right of the river that flowed past at the end. My mother had us out picking up sticks for the range down its dappled, dusty length in the mottled sunlight of a warm summer's afternoon, away from the tarmacked road of my cousins' village.

She walked on ahead of us and my six cousins and me followed, picking up sticks as we went. My mother had us all singing, working our way through 'One Man Went To Mow'. The gang of mowers had grown to seven, when we heard a noise. My mother, a pile of sticks in her two arms as if she was cradling a delicate baby, stopped.

We all stopped too.

The noise came again, louder this time, the sound of twigs breaking underfoot.

"Halt!" cried my mother. "Who goes there, friend or foe?"

A boy about my own age came running out of the shadows.

"It's Granny!" he said, breathing hard. "I can't wake her. I need to get to the McEntees' shop to phone for an ambulance."

"Is that Mrs Kelly?" asked my mother.

"It is," he said.

A look came over my mother's face.

"Quick!" she said to Johnny and Geraldine. "Go with this lad and get that ambulance here as fast you can. Go on! Run!"

Johnny and Geraldine threw down their sticks and started sprinting off with the boy. I watched Johnny pull ahead of them and then turned to see my mother running the other way, her own big bundle of sticks abandoned also, the speed of her amazing me.

"Come on!" shouted Mattie. "Let's go!"

The rest of my cousins and me all ran after her, the dapples and the sunlight kaleidoscoping through the trees as we sprinted. My mother was a good ten yards ahead of us now, her bare legs and white sandals a blur as she flew down the lane. After a good hard couple of hundred yards my mother was nowhere to be seen, Mattie was ahead of us, and a cottage just beyond him stood amidst a small copse of trees at the end of the long lane.

We caught up with Mattie. He was standing outside the cottage, waiting for us.

"Come on," he said. He pushed the front door open and we followed him inside.

Everything was quiet, a gloom from the trees dimming the front room. It took a while to get used to the lack of light, but Mattie had spotted the way to Mrs Kelly's bedroom. He was tiptoeing towards the open door where I could just make out the shadowy outline of my mother kneeling at Mrs Kelly's bedside, holding her hand.

"Is that you Mary?" Mrs Kelly's voice was very faint, like a voice coming from the darkness outside. We all stood at the door, watching in silence.

"It's me," said my mother. "The ambulance is on the way. Don't talk – it's going to be all right."

"I'm ready, Mary," said Mrs Kelly. "God will take me soon enough. I know my time has come – I prayed you'd be here."

It was hard to tell but it seemed to me my mother was crying.

"It was very sad the time your mother died," said Mrs Kelly in her faint voice. "And you so young. I remember like it was yesterday – your poor father was destroyed."

In the distance I could hear the rumble of a motor, the crunch of gravel and sticks. The ambulance – it must be very close now.

"You were very little then. Three, weren't you? Your brother

Tommy wasn't much older, and Annie was what? A year younger? Your father couldn't cope. My father said he saw him in McKenna's pub, a feed of drink in him, his head on the counter of the bar, sobbing his heart out. So I asked my father if we could help."

"Don't," said my mother. "Save your breath. I can hear the ambulance coming. It's nearly here."

"It doesn't matter, Mary. I don't have long, but I'm glad you've come."

The old woman's voice was little more than a whisper now, but in the darkness of the room I could hear every word.

"I loved your father so much. That's what I wanted to tell you. I asked him to marry me, but he said he couldn't, that he was devoted to the memory of your mother. He said he didn't want to put another mother over you to drive out any affection, any love, you had for her."

The track outside the cottage crunched and rattled as the wheels of a vehicle rolled forward. I could hear footsteps running towards the open door, and soon they were in the room.

"Granny! Granny!" shouted the boy.

My uncle stood behind him with Johnny and Geraldine.

"Is she gone?" he asked.

My mother rose slowly from the bedside. She smoothed down the folds of her summer dress, her face half in shadow.

"She is, Tommy."

The boy burst into tears. He ran forwards and knelt by her bed.

"She was a good woman," said my uncle.

"She was," said my mother.

In the distance I could hear a siren. We stood for a moment, the old lady's grandson sobbing by her bed, then turned and walked outside.

I thought then of the range, of the sticks lying scattered all over the lane. I shivered a little and at last the ambulance came and the grown-ups moved slowly to one side.

The Goat

What we need is a goat," said Uncle Tommy.

He stuck a fork into the big bowl of potatoes in the middle of the table and pulled out a spud. He peeled it with his knife, paring off the floury skin, letting the flaky speckled peels fall into a dish beside his plate.

"A goat will keep that grass down out the back and we'll be able to milk it as well. And we might even get a stew out of it."

He grinned and laid the steaming potato on his plate next to slices of boiled ham and glistening cabbage.

"A goat, Tommy?" said Auntie Lizzie. "Are you sure? They can be dangerous articles. Sure Ellie had a goat and it near drove her mad."

"Well, it won't be driving me mad," said Uncle Tommy. "You've just got to show a goat who's boss. It'll cost nothing to feed, and no sweat to look after."

Mattie and me rattled down the gravel driveway on our bikes. We swerved round the far corner of the house and came to a halt by the big red corrugated iron shed at the back.

"Come on," said Matt. "Let's go and get a look at her."

We lent the bikes up against the shed and strolled off towards the garden. Uncle Tommy had planted all sorts of stuff out the back. Really it was more like a small field than a garden, about the size of a football pitch, with rows of carrots, potatoes, cabbages, and peas laid out across the big plot nearest to the house. He'd also planted a couple of trees at about the halfway line, with apples sweeter than you'd get in the shop. At the far end, running down to the riverbank, was a large expanse of long grass, wildflowers, and weeds, and it was here the goat stood, chomping away in the sunshine.

We walked down the path by the tall bush that separated Uncle Tommy's house from the McEntees, beside all the rows of carrots and cabbages, the peas and potatoes, and on past the two apple trees on the far side. We turned and cut through the long grass till we were about ten feet from the goat. She raised her head to look at us.

"She's the quare one," said Matt.

The goat was on a long rusty chain tethered to a small stake sticking out of the ground amongst all the grass and wildflowers and weeds. Her mild eyes, unblinking in the sunshine, were what you noticed first. They were like large yellow marbles, with a wisp of iris in them, horizontal and dark, the eyes of an alien, like a creature's from outer space. Then you saw the ears, sticking out like handles, as white as the rest of her.

I took a step forward.

"What are you doing?" said Matt.

"Saying hello," I said. And I patted the goat on her forehead.

"Watch out!" he cried. "She'll have the hand off you!"

But the goat didn't move. She just stood there, enjoying the attention.

"There's a good goat," I said, my voice soft and soothing. "You wouldn't have my hand off, will you? You've enough to eat here, haven't you, Billy?"

I don't where the name came from – the fairy story about the Three Billy Goats Gruff I suppose. But it seemed to suit her.

"Do you want to say hello yourself?" I asked my cousin.

I looked around but Matt was gone, back down the path, turning once to scowl at me, and into the house.

I turned back to Billy. It was very peaceful there, just the two us in the long grass, and I told her again what a good goat she was as she chomped away. A while later my mother called me from the door of the kitchen. I murmured my goodbyes to Billy and walked slowly down the pathway, ready now for my dinner.

"What do you think of her boys?"

Uncle Tommy looked at us across the table. I was hoping he would hurry up peeling his potato. It was poised in mid-air on the end of his fork, steam rising out of it, a warm earthy smell wafting towards me.

"She's a fine creature," said Matt.

I said nothing. Matt had changed his tune, I thought.

"What about you, John Kevin? What do you think of the goat?"

I looked at Uncle Tommy.

"I think she's very friendly," I said.

"Friendly?" said Uncle Tommy. "She's not a pet, John Kevin. She's a means to an end."

I wasn't sure what he meant. A means to an end? I dropped my eyes to his potato. It was a large one, the skin just coming apart to reveal the soft white flesh inside.

Uncle Tommy started peeling the spud, making brisk work of it, the peels dropping into the little dish as he went.

"That's the thing with an English gossoon like you," said Matt. "You think all animals are pets. You'd make a dote of a donkey."

"No, I wouldn't," I said.

"Sure goats are in his blood," said my mother. "Hurry up with the spuds, would you, Tommy?"

Uncle Tommy drew out another and began peeling, a little quicker this time.

"What do you mean, Auntie Mary, 'in his blood'?" said Matt. "Is John Kevin part goat himself?"

The rest of my cousins started snickering, but my mother waited till they had stopped.

"Wait till he butts you with that head Matthew Murphy and you'll soon know, you cheeky pup. Have you never heard of Puck Fair?"

"Puck Fair?" said Matt. "What's that?"

"It's a big hooley down in Killorglin where his father is from. Goes on for four days and four nights, the pubs open all the time, and then they crown a goat King of Puck Fair."

"And what do they do then?" said Matt. "Marry him off to the Rose of Tralee?"

The snickering turned now to laughter.

"That's enough," said Uncle Tommy sharply.

Everyone fell silent.

From outside I was sure I could hear Billy chomping away. My mother said I could hear the grass grow. Sometimes I thought I did hear a faint rustling when I was walking in a meadow but this was louder. Good old Billy, I thought. Get your fill. One day I'll crown you and take you to meet the King of Puck Fair. Mattie won't call me an English gossoon then. For I'll be a proper Kerryman like my father, and if you call me names I'll set the goat on you.

"Don't be afraid of her. She won't bite."

Uncle Tommy walked towards Billy, me and my six cousins a few steps behind him. I think if she'd let a noise out of her they would have all have gone pop. But I wasn't scared of her. I thought she was a nice goat, and when she caught my eye I smiled. In the blazing dazzle of sunlight it looked as if she smiled back.

"Now all we have to do is get this stool under her, and then the bucket, and then work away at the milking. Watch me and then you can try yourselves."

We were now about five feet from Billy, Uncle Tommy in front, his white shirt open at the neck, his great black trousers hanging off his big belly, the stool in one hand, the red plastic bucket in the other. He sat on the stool and placed the bucket under the goat. He reached out for her, and turned round to smile at us.

"You see?" he said. "That's all there is to it."

Billy shifted towards him while he was looking round and leapt up on him. Over Uncle Tommy went, toppling off his stool and sprawling backwards into the weeds. She turned round, took a step forward and kicked over the bucket with her hind leg. Then she returned to her chomping as if nothing had happened.

I tried not to laugh.

"Are you all right, Daddy?" cried Anna.

Uncle Tommy got up and righted the stool.

"I'm fine, I'm fine," he said. "She's playing with me, Anna. Let's try it again. Watch closely now."

"Be careful, Daddy!" Anna looked anxious.

Uncle Tommy picked up the stool in one hand and the bucket in another and took a step towards Billy. She had her back to him now, as if she was ignoring him. He placed the stool beside her and planted the bucket under her. Billy walked calmly forward, knocking the bucket over again.

"Matt!" said Uncle Tommy, twisting round.

He was getting cross now.

"Yes, Daddy?" said Matt.

"Catch a hold of her!"

"What about John Kevin, Daddy?" said Matt. "He likes the goat. She wouldn't put up a fight with him. Couldn't he catch a hold of her?"

Uncle Tommy turned to me.

"Well, John Kevin?" he said. "Would you get a grip of the goat while I try and milk her?"

I looked at Billy. She seemed so peaceful there in the sunshine, chomping away at the long grass, enjoying the weeds and wildflowers.

"Why don't I milk her?" I said. "I think she's a bit afraid of you, Uncle Tommy."

He looked at me, his eyes narrowing a little.

"So why isn't she afraid of you, John Kevin?"

Uncle Tommy sounded suspicious. But I liked Billy, that was all. There was something about her eyes, her mild manner, the way she seemed to smile at me, that drew me to her. I liked talking to her and stroking her forehead and watching her chew away at the long grass.

"I don't know why she's not afraid of me," I said. "But I think she'll let me milk her."

Uncle Tommy stepped aside. I took up the stool that was lying in the grass and placed it near her. I sat down and put the bucket under her teats.

"Now, Billy," I said softly. "Will you be a good goat so I can milk you? We just want a bit of milk then we'll leave you alone for the day. Now what do you say?"

Billy chomped and chomped but I could tell she was happy to hear me talking. She wouldn't knock me off the stool or kick the bucket over and walk away. I think it was because I was a lot smaller than Uncle Tommy. He must have seemed like a big bear to her.

Once I was settled I reached out for her teats. I thought the milk in them would have made them cooler, but they were actually quite warm. I pulled on two of them gently but firmly, and the milk started shooting into the bucket.

My cousins gasped.

I took no notice. It seemed to me the most natural thing in the world, squeezing Billy's teats on a warm summer's day, milk sloshing around the bucket, rising by inches as I dragged and pulled.

I worked away until I had the bucket half full, a froth of bubbles on top of the milk. It must have taken me about five minutes but I was sort of lost in the rhythm of it, in a kind of trance, so I wasn't too sure how long I'd been at it.

"Will that be enough?" I asked Uncle Tommy, tipping the bucket so he could see how much there was.

He bent down and caught the bucket by the white plastic handle, turned, and walked off in silence with it back to the house.

Gradually my cousins stopped staring at me and followed him.

We rolled into the back yard, Uncle Tommy's Morris Minor full to bursting, and pulled up by the big red corrugated iron shed. My aunt and uncle got out first followed by the rest of us. It was a relief to be standing in the noonday sunshine.

"He says a quick Mass, that Fr Ryan," said my mother.

"Sure the Last Supper itself was over in half an hour," said Uncle Tommy. "What was good enough for Our Lord is surely good enough the curate of St Mary's." He smiled and walked towards the house. He pushed open the kitchen door and let out a shout.

"What the hell is going on in here?" he cried.

We all rushed to the door to see what was happening. In the kitchen Billy was nibbling a cauliflower on the lino.

Uncle Tommy advanced.

She looked up at him, those mild, alien eyes taking him in. Then she charged forward, catching him hard in the stomach. He fell and she skipped over him.

Geraldine, Mary, Evelyn, and Anna let out a scream and scattered back before her. Billy scampered into the yard and on up the path to the back garden. My mother and Auntie Lizzie rushed towards Uncle Tommy. He looked as if Henry Cooper had given him a left hook.

"Are you all right, Tommy?" said my aunt.

"I'm fine, I'm fine," he said, leaning on my mother and Auntie Lizzie as he got to his feet. "Where's that bloody animal? I'll kill her!"

The three of them came to the door of the kitchen. The girls were cowering by the wall of the house, holding on to each other and whimpering. Johnny, Matt, and myself had gone out into the yard and were looking down towards the back garden.

Billy was by the apple trees and looked back at us. Uncle Tommy marched off towards her.

"Come on," he said. "We need to teach that bucking goat a lesson."

My aunt and my mother followed behind him down the path. Johnny, Matt, and me chased after them. The girls were torn between obeying their father and holding on to life and limb. At last they too came walking down the path, still clutching at one another, Evelyn and Anna whimpering the closer they got to Billy.

Up ahead Uncle Tommy had stopped.

He was flanked by Auntie Lizzie and my mother, us boys behind them. The girls were about ten feet further back. Everything was still for a moment.

Then Uncle Tommy charged.

Billy waited until he was three feet from her then ran to her right towards the big hedge separating us from the McEntees.

"Don't let her down the path!" yelled my uncle.

The girls all ran screaming back to the house, scared out of their wits.

Johnny and Matt ran to cut her off and blocked the path. They crouched low and spread out their hands, as if they were shaping to save a goal. I stood watching it all, not knowing what to think.

Uncle Tommy came round the back of Billy now, and Auntie Lizzie and my mother were in a line with him. Poor Billy would be caught between them if she didn't make a smart move soon.

Seeing Johnny and Matt on the path she turned round. Uncle Tommy was nearly upon her. I couldn't see her knocking him over again. He would be up to that trick now. What was Billy going to do?

She suddenly ran forward. I could see what was in her mind. There was a two foot gap between Uncle Tommy and the big hedge at the side of the path – she might just get through if she was quick.

Uncle Tommy also twigged what Billy was thinking. It was like watching a nippy winger up against a full back with a grudge. Uncle Tommy made a dash for the gap. She ran as fast as light and desperate now Uncle Tommy dived.

I watched open-mouthed as he sailed through the air only to miss Billy who stood watching him. Then she ran up the path and away.

"Tommy! Are you hurt?"

Auntie Lizzie dashed across to him.

But he wasn't thinking of his bruises.

He was staring at Billy, down by the very end of the garden at the river.

"That bucking goat!" he said.

He got up and dusted himself off.

"Come on. We'll corner her by the river. This time we have her. She can only go sideways or forwards."

He turned round and called Johnny and Matt.

"Boys! Come on up here to we catch her. I'll get her head on, and you boys and Mammy and Auntie Mary can catch her at the side. The only way out is the river. We have her trapped."

As he turned back he caught sight of me.

He looked at me as if I was in league with Billy. In a way I was. I didn't want anyone to hurt her. I wanted her to get away.

But what could I do?

They started closing in on her now, my uncle walking slowly forwards, Johnny and Matt at the very top of the path where it petered out in the grass, Auntie Lizzie and my mother coming at her the other way.

My uncle was two feet from Billy. My cousins and my aunt and my mother were in position. She was cornered.

"I have you now!" roared Uncle Tommy.

He lurched forward. Billy turned and jumped into the river. I didn't know goats could swim and nor, it seemed, did Uncle Tommy. She swam away in the sunshine as he teetered on the edge of the river. His arms started windmilling backwards but it was too late. He slowly inclined towards the water, arms akimbo, and seemed to freeze for a moment like that, until suddenly he fell forward. There was an almighty splash and a great spume of spray rose from the river as Uncle Tommy hit the surface.

I ran forwards.

As I got to the water's edge my worst fears all came true.

Billy was nowhere to be seen.

Jimmy McCormack rescued her later that afternoon. She'd swum downstream and got caught in some riverweeds. He was driving home from seeing his brother in Scotsville when he saw her struggling in the water. He knew straight away Billy belonged to Uncle Tommy. It was Jimmy who'd sold Billy to him. So when I saw Jimmy pull up in his van with Billy my heart leapt. Billy was safe! I almost ran out of the kitchen and threw my arms round her.

Then I saw my uncle and Jimmy McCormack talking. I don't know what Uncle Tommy said but Jimmy McCormack got back in his van and drove off with her.

It turned out that Uncle Tommy said Billy was too wild, that he couldn't control her, that only I had could control her, and I'd be away back to England before the summer was over and then what would they do.

That's as much as anyone would tell me.

I have my own idea about what happened.

I think she escaped again and ran away to Kerry and the King of Puck Fair where they lived happily ever after up in the wild mountains of the West.

But that's only a daydream.

And I'm only an English gossoon who should know better.

But I loved Billy, her mild eyes, the understanding we had, the peace that passed between us.

And now she's gone.

The Time Capsule

We were walking down to JonJo's when I got the idea.

"What about a Time Capsule?"

My cousins looked baffled.

"They had one on Blue Peter," I said. "What you do is put objects in a box and bury it. Then thirty years later you dig it up again."

"What's the point of that, John Kevin?" asked Mary.

We'd all arrived at the creamery and I stopped and looked at the familiar white walls, the red corrugated iron roof. My cousins all stopped too and followed my gaze.

"The point is," I said, "to take a snapshot of the present. Take this creamery. The way things are going, with men on the Moon and rockets to Mars before you know it, in thirty years' time there may not even be a creamery."

"So how will we get our milk?" asked Matt.

"Who knows?" I asked. "But thirty years ago no one around here was even thinking of going to the Moon. By the time we're all grown up there'll be a new century, a new millennium, and milk might come in tablets, or be injected into you, or we might even not need food at all. We might be on different planets, and fixed in such a way we could live on the atmosphere."

"And pigs might fly," said Matt.

"Ah, come on, Matt," I said. "It'll be fun. We'll be like pirates burying treasure, and only we will have the map. Then in the Year

2000 we can all meet and dig up the Time Capsule and see what's in it."

"But we'll know what's in it," said Mary.

"We might have forgotten," I said. "Anyway, we won't be kids forever, and by the Year 2000 we might all be wondering what it was like to have been young. We'll all be ancient by then. As old as my mother, as old as your mother and father, as Jonjo, and the Handleys, and the McEntees."

They all fell silent for a moment. I could see them trying to look into the future, to imagine themselves as adults, married maybe, perhaps with families of their own, working away in jobs like Uncle Tommy in the Post Office, or Auntie Lizzie in the nursing before she was married, or gone to England, like my mother and father, or even further afield.

"What we put in the Time Capsule will remind us, will take us back to today, to here and now, as surely as a Time Machine could," I said. "We'll be sending ourselves a message to the future, and when we dig up the Time Capsule, we'll be communicating with the past. We can travel through space, but we can't travel through time. But we'll have the next best thing. We'll be able to travel back to today thirty years from now. We'll be chrononauts."

That did the trick.

They all agreed to put something in the Time Capsule, and after we'd got back from Jonjo's, ice creams all eaten, we set to work.

Jonjo gave us what we needed. It was a smallish wooden box, with black lettering on the lid that said *Bushmills*. He told us a salesman had given it to him, that it had contained a couple of bottles of whiskey, a thank you to Jonjo for being such a loyal customer over the years. This was to be our Time Capsule.

"OK," I said. We were all in my cousins' bedroom, the six beds facing each other in two rows of three. I was sitting on Matt's bed, the *Bushmills* box on his faded red counterpane, him sitting alongside me.

The rest of them crowded round, looking at the Time Capsule as if it were a crystal ball.

"OK," I said. "What have we got?"

Johnny spoke first.

"I've got a Corgi car. But not just any Corgi car. This is James Bond's Aston Martin DB5, from *Goldfinger*."

He leaned over and handed it to me. There was a tire gone off one of the front wheels, and the little blue man in the ejector seat was missing, but otherwise it looked all right.

"And why the car, Johnny?" I asked him.

"Because one day when I'm grown up I'm going to have a car just like James Bond and be a secret agent." He started singing the theme tune, swinging around with an imaginary gun like 007 in the films' opening titles.

"OK," I said, laughing. "In it goes."

I laid the car in the box and looked round.

"Well," I said. "What about you, Geraldine?"

She held up a set of Rosary beads.

"Auntie Aggie gave me these for my First Holy Communion. I want to make sure they're in a safe place. If they go into the box I'll always know where they are."

She leaned over and handed me the beads. I took them from her and laid them carefully next to Johnny's car. Then it was Matt's turn.

"Well," I said. "What have you got, coz?"

He leaned over and from under his bed took out something I couldn't quite see. He hauled himself up, whatever it was in his hand.

"The Man of Steel himself," he said, brandishing a Superman comic. "Very hard to get these, John Kevin. Only you sent them over I don't think I'd even have heard of Clark Kent. So I'm storing this away to remember the two of us and the summers we've had together."

I looked at Matt and took the comic from him. We both loved superheroes. Only in America could you find men and women with superpowers – only the Yanks had the kind of bold imagination needed to think up characters like that. Superman was the best though – he was the King. That's why Matt and I liked him so much.

I carefully rolled up the comic and put it in the box.

"What about you, Mary?" I said.

She fished out an envelope from under her pillow.

"It's a letter, John Kevin. A letter to my future self."

I wondered what she'd written but said nothing. Letters were supposed to be private after all.

I took the letter from her and placed it in the box.

Evelyn was next.

"Well, Evelyn," I said. "What do you want to put in the Time Capsule?"

Evelyn held up a photo.

"This is us in Blackrock, the day Daddy drove us down to Dublin. I think it'll remind us all of the fun we had that afternoon."

I thanked Evelyn and laid the photo in the box. It was starting to fill up.

"What about you, Anna?" I said.

Anna reached over and pulled up a bag stuffed full of toys and books by her bed. She brought out an old doll I thought I recognised.

"What about Dolly, John Kevin? Could I get her in?"

I looked at the doll. It was the one with no arms and only one eye I remembered from when we were little.

"I think she's a bit too big," I said.

Johnny reached over and snatched the doll out of her hand.

"Here, Anna," he said. He wrenched a leg off of Dolly. "Now. That'll go in without any fuss."

"Ach, Johnny!" cried Anna. "You've destroyed Dolly! You've amputated her leg!"

She snatched up the doll and held her close to her chest.

"Now, now, Dolly," she said. "Don't worry, Mammy will look after you."

"Sure that doll was destroyed before I ever took her leg off, Anna," said Johnny. "No arms, only one eye – she's a wreck."

"Don't say that about Dolly!" cried Anna. "She's my pet and I love her."

We all looked at each other, not sure how seriously we should take Anna.

"Will I put the doll in?" I asked her gently.

"Ach, you might as well, John Kevin," she said. "Sure she's destroyed now right enough."

Anna handed me the doll and I laid it in the box.

It was my turn.

"I have a book," I said. It lay in front on me on Matt's faded counterpane, the red cover garish against the washed out material.

"It's *Just William*," I said. "My favourite."

And I put *Just William* in the box along with all the other objects, Johnny's car, Geraldine's Rosary beads, Matt's Superman comic, Mary's letter, Evelyn's photo, Anna's doll.

"Right," I said. "Where shall we bury it?"

We were out beyond Ballydawn, the day still fresh and warm. I carried the Time Capsule in my duffle bag, and walked in front of my cousins, who were all in a line behind me. It was the first time I had ever walked at the front and I felt very important.

"Not long now," said Johnny.

"O'Reilly's field is down there after the road forks," said Matt. "The cottage has been tumbledown this years, ever since he want to America."

"Doesn't anyone own the place?" I asked.

"If they do they're not around much," said Johnny. "I heard rumours that O'Reilly wouldn't sell up because of some secret to do with the place, but I reckon that's only fairy stories."

"So why didn't O'Reilly sell then?" I asked.

"Perhaps he never thought he'd be gone so long. Perhaps he's dead and never coming back," said Johnny.

We walked on in silence. It felt a bit eerie to be going to a place that had been abandoned. But Johnny and Matt had decided.

A couple of cars passed us as we came to the fork in the road, then we bore left and after a couple of hundred yards I saw the cottage. It lay a good bit back from the ditch, in more of a field than a front garden. The roof was in and the windows were boarded up, which I thought strange. Someone had obviously been along and taken care of them, but the roof looked like it was beyond care. There was a gloomy old air to the place, as if whatever soul it may once have had had long ago departed. It was no longer a home, just a piece of property. It felt like a forlorn place for a Time Capsule. But I suppose if no one was interested in O'Reilly's field our treasured possessions would be safe.

"Come on," said Johnny, and he hopped over the low-lying wall in one quick leap. Matt followed and then they helped the rest of us.

"Here'll do as well as anywhere," said Johnny.

"Shouldn't we go up nearer the cottage?" said Matt.

"If ever anyone knocks it down and builds on it they'll come across the box," said Johnny. "No – this should be as good a place as any. Have you Daddy's trowel, John Kevin?"

I laid down my duffle bag and took the trowel out of it. Johnny grabbed it from me and soon set to work. Within a few minutes he had dug a hole about six inches deep. Then the trowel knocked against something. Something solid.

"Hold on." he said. "What's this?."

We all crouched over, straining to see what the trowel had hit. Johnny scraped away a layer of dirt to reveal the slats of a long box lying in the ground.

"Looks like someone beat us to it," said Johnny. He stood up, the trowel in his hand, and looked down at the box. He had uncovered most of the length of it, about three feet I reckoned, far bigger than the Time Capsule.

"What's in it?" said Matt, peering into the shallow rectangle Johnny had dug.

"Only one way to find out," he said. He bent down again and laid the trowel to one side. He grabbed the long box and lifted it out of the ground, laying it on the grass beside the hole. Then he snatched up the trowel and levered the lid off in two sharp yanks at the side of it, the damp wood coming away easy. There were sharp intakes of breath when we saw what was inside.

A rifle.

"What do we now?" asked Matt.

"Nothing," said Johnny. He put the lid back on the box and laid it in the earth again. Quickly he filled in the hole and smoothed the black earth back over. He stood up and looked at us all. Dusk was falling, and I felt a sudden shiver as he stood with his back to the fading light.

"We do nothing, we say nothing," he said. "Whatever this gun is, whoever buried it here, is none of our business. It wasn't so long ago this country was at war. The way things are going in the North there might be war again before you know it. So we keep quiet about this. Come on. Let's get out of here."

He climbed back over the wall and we all followed him, away from O'Reilly's field and whatever secrets were buried there. As we walked back in silence I realised then that all my talk of being a time traveller was foolishness. I knew nothing of Ireland's past, I was only here at all because of my mother, an English boy pretending I belonged. The world she had lived in would never be my world.

I carried the *Bushmills* box back to my cousins' house. It was dud now, lumber, junk, something that would end up in Auntie Lizzie's range along with the sticks we picked up down Clintock's Lane and the timber Matt sawed in the back yard.

We came over the bridge and past the creamery.

Night was falling fast and the trinkets in the box rattled faintly as I walked.

Playing Tig

I ran through the trees, the light colliding off the branches and leaves as I went. Mary was on it and she was chasing me. But I was good at dodging – I swerved and tilted and then I was running along by the river, Mary trailing away behind.

The rest were all whooping and hollering. "Run John Kevin!". "Watch out!". "Don't let her catch you!". But I knew I was too good to be caught. I was a nippy lad, that was what my mother said. I might be a bit smaller than Mattie but if he was on it he wouldn't have been able to catch me either. Because I had the beating of him too.

It felt great to be nippy. I was flying now. I felt like I was running a four minute mile, like I was made of speed and light.

"Tig!"

I felt a hand on my back.

Mary.

Rats!

Here in the woods the sun falls dappled through the leaves of the trees and glints on the rippling river. It's cooler by the water, away from the dusty road and the village. The patterns of sunlight are like webs, spread out across the trees and falling on the ground and the little flowers, deckling the leaves and making the petals – purple, yellow, white – glow. It's as if the light has been sieved, as if it's been filtered of brightness in this bosky forest: the woods, the canopy of branches and leaves, the cooling river, all shade us from the heat, the bright sunshine falling on this backcountry scene.

There are some tracks through the woods, where leaves lie mulched with twigs on the dark earth, and down one of these tracks we've all come. Geraldine, Mattie, Mary, Evelyn, Anna, and me. Johnny is away somewhere, wherever teenagers go, off with his pals swimming, or riding around on Rory McDermott's motorbike, or perhaps away up to Town. He's getting bigger now, closer in some ways to the grown-ups than he is to us.

I wonder if my mother ever came here when she was a girl, who she played with, what she got up to. It's strange to think of her as a girl – she's always been part of that grown-up world my father and my aunt and uncle live in, that all grown-ups live in. A world I sometimes get glimpses of but that I feel is somehow mysterious, different from the world of my cousins and my friends.

For now, though, we are miles away from that world, almost from the world itself.

"Have you had a good summer, John Kevin?" says Mary.

We are all sitting cross-legged by the river, taking a rest from playing Tig. A few dragonflies, bright and gaudy in their purple fuselages, hover over the river, then zoom off.

"The best," I say.

"Summer wouldn't be summer without Auntie Mary and John Kevin coming over," says Geraldine.

"Maybe one day we'll all come over to London," says Mattie.

I think of our flat, how tiny it is compared to my aunt and uncle's bungalow.

"Maybe," I say.

"Could we, John Kevin?" asks Anna.

"I'll have to ask my mother," I say.

"What about your father?" says Mattie. "Wouldn't you have to ask him as well?"

I think of my father, and wonder what is he up to, and why he never comes to Ballydawn. I think there may have been a feud, or perhaps he's not so keen on Monaghan, being from the other end of the country. Or maybe his job won't give him the time off work.

And then I have another thought.

I think back to the first time I can remember my mother and me coming over. I think about the row they had, the two of them blazing away at each other. I see my father again, my mother telling him we're leaving, him asking me to stay.

Perhaps this is the reason my father never comes over.

Perhaps he feels I've betrayed him, that I am a Judas, that I hurt him all those years ago.

I miss him then.

And the missing is mixed with guilt.

"My father?" I say quietly. "I'm sure he wouldn't mind."

I try to put my fears about my father to the back of my mind. I tell myself there's nothing I can do here. And anyway, why is he always so kind to me? Why did he send those autographs, call me John Boy, bring me chocolate when he comes in from work?

Surely he loves me?

Mary snatches up a few stalks of long grass from a clump down beside her. I watch fascinated as she starts to work them together, folding, plaiting corners, manipulating the long green blades of grass until she has made a little box with a door.

"There," she says, holding her box of stalks up for us all to see. "A grasshopper cage."

I'm amazed but the rest pass no remark.

Anna looks as if she doesn't want to be upstaged. So softly, slowly she starts singing a song:

> Dearest fairbrown and faithful, most silken of cows,
>> Where do you wander by night and by day?
> Oh, I wander the woods, far from any fine house,
>> Bereft of the beauty who's left me astray.
>
> I am landless and homeless, without music or wine,
>> This forest for company, the wind and the birds,
> Lost in the land where no sun ever shines,
>> Far from my hearth and fairbrown faithful herds.
>
> But if I could speak, or wore a bright crown,
>> The Saxon I'd break and this I avow

I'd run him from hillside and river and town
    Singing the while to my fairbrown old cow.

"That's a nice song," I say. "Where did you get that one, Anna?

"It's an old Irish poem," says Anna. "I had to put it into English for my ecker."

"And where did you get the tune?"

"It's a slow air Daddy plays in the Fleadh Ceol."

There's a silence, as the soft melody of Anna's song drifts away from us.

"I'm going to play for Manchester United," says Mattie at last. "Just like Georgie Boy. And I'm going to be a winger – just like him. And win the European Cup – just like him!"

Mattie gets up and starts kicking an invisible football. He swerves, ducks, shimmies, shoots.

"Goal!" he cries. "A wonderful shot by this fine young talent from Ireland, Matthew Murphy, the new Best, Charlton, and Law, all rolled into one. In fact this lad could be even better than them. I've never seen anything like him!"

"Ach, would you sit down and shut up about football," says Geraldine. "Fr Casey is very sick and here's you crowing about Georgie Best."

"What odds if I crow or if I don't? You think crowing is going to make him worse?"

"Perhaps if you thought of saying a prayer for him," says Geraldine, "it would be more your style."

"That's what I'm going to do when I'm older," says Evelyn.

"Pray for Fr Ryan?" says Mattie. "Sure if you listen to her he could be dead by then."

"I'm going to be a nurse," says Evelyn. "And help sick people."

"I think we should say a few prayers for Fr Ryan ," says Geraldine. Mattie gives her a look but we all kneel down and say an Our Father and a Hail Mary for the priest, and as I'm saying the prayers with my cousins dusk starts to fall.

I think of my father in London, and ask God to make him love me, that when we return all will be well between us, that one year he'll come over for the holidays.

It's the last summer of the decade, 1969. Soon it will be 1970. I'm 11 now. I realise that this is the last summer of my childhood. In the autumn I'll be off to secondary school, to Cardinal Wiseman, in long trousers and a blazer. I'll get homework, and there'll be new teachers, new kids coming from other schools, new roads to walk to get there.

These summers I've had – they're coming to an end. I'm not sure how, but I'm aware that a special time in my young life is ending. I used to be a carefree boy roaming around the country with my cousins, with Mattie and the rest. But it's coming to some kind of close. The day that's ending, the summer nearly over, the Sixties themselves...

Whatever future that lies ahead will be different from now on.

We walk home in silence, through Ballydawn, past the garage with the red door, JonJo's shop, the Handley Brothers' cottage, on up to the bridge, past Maggie's bar, the creamery, night falling now, the stars starting to prick the black velvet spread of space, and then the final few hundred yards to my aunt and uncle's bungalow.

I try to take everything in, to fix it in my memory, but the deepening darkness means that I can't make out clearly the colours, the textures of cottage walls with their stipples of whitewash, the red of the garage door, the signs for ice cream outside JonJo's shop, the shade of brown paint the door of Maggie's bar is done in, the contours of the corrugated iron roof on the creamery, the fixtures on the gates of the bungalows we pass.

It's as if all is vanishing into the night, as if this lovely world I have known every summer of my life, this place my mother calls home, is strange to me, cold, dark, and mine no more.

We arrive home.

"Terrible news," says my mother.

"What is it, Auntie Mary?" cries Anna.

"It's the North," says Uncle Tommy. He's sitting at the table, shirt open at the neck, a shocked look on his face. "There's been terrible scenes in Belfast and Derry. People have been injured, houses set on fire, and there's reports of killings as well."

"It's war," says my mother grimly. "Bloody war."

We look at each other, my cousins and me. I'd been over the Border earlier that summer, smuggling butter, but I sense that what my mother and uncle is talking about is further away.

"Sure it's been coming for years," says my aunt. She's by the range, lighting a fag, looking as grim as my mother and my uncle.

"Will there be fighting round here?" says Geraldine.

"God forbid," says my aunt.

Everyone falls silent.

Then my uncle says, "Where's Johnny?"

No one knows. Now the atmosphere in the room changes. It's almost like something you can reach out and touch.

"It's not safe," says my uncle. "I'm going off to look for him."

He goes out and we hear him start the car, the wheels crunching on the gravel as he drives off.

My aunt comes and sits at the table where Uncle Tommy has been sitting.

"Don't worry, Lizzie" says my mother. "They'll both be back soon enough."

We all fall quiet, just the ticking of the grandfather clock breaking the silence.

And then we hear the gravel crunch again, and we rush to the window to see who it is. The latch of the door lifts and there are footsteps in the kitchen.

"Well," says Johnny, coming into the room. "You're all up late. What's going on?"

"Have you not heard?" says Auntie Lizzie. "Belfast and the Bogside are up in flames."

"How come?" says Johnny.

"Riots," says my mother.

"Sweet Jesus!" says Johnny. "Anyone hurt?"

"Plenty," says my aunt. "There's injured and there's dead as well."

"Where's Daddy?" says Johnny.

"Out looking for you," says Auntie Lizzie.

We all fall quiet again.

"Come on," says my mother to me at last. "It's time for your bed."

I go and brush my teeth, and then I go to our room.

What's happening? What does it all mean? Is Ireland going to be a war zone, like Vietnam? Will the Yanks send soldiers over to keep the peace? Will we get back to England before the war comes to Ballydawn?

I want to ask my mother all of these questions. But she's gone back to the front room to wait for my uncle. I hear a radio being turned on, a reporter describing what he can see.

And then I start to fall asleep, the radio still going, my father far away in England, blackness at last all around.

A Wedding

We left the church, the bells ringing loudly in our ears, confetti on the steps, a fleet of black saloons gleaming in the sunshine down by the roadside.

"This one here," said my uncle, ushering us towards the back seat of a Ford Zephyr. We got in beside Auntie Lizzie in the back and Uncle Tommy went in the front. The car sped off, the country roads more or less empty as we glided towards the Glen View Hotel.

"I like a good wedding." said my mother. "They always make me cry."

"Me too," said Auntie Lizzie.

"Ach, don't be daft," said my uncle. "Sure the cost is the only reason to cry over a wedding. This one's costing Gusty a fortune."

Gusty was Auntie Lizzie's cousin and it was Gusty's daughter, Nuala, who'd got married. She was an only child, and Auntie Lizzie said Gusty wanted to make this the wedding of the year. She looked very beautiful at the altar, and Michael, her husband, was handsome too, in his smart suit, collar-length dark hair and sideburns, a hint of Georgie Best about him.

"We're here," said Uncle Tommy as we turned into the Glen View. We all got out of the car and headed off towards the entrance. Behind us, Johnny pulled up in his MG. My mother told me he'd won it off of Packie McIlvanney at cards. He'd grown up since we were last over, eighteen now, as tall as his father, dapper in a smart double-breasted grey suit, white shirt with a large pointy collar and big blue glossy kipper tie, out at dances and chasing girls, driving his new car like Jackie Stewart over the drumlins, coming home at all hours.

"Well, John Kevin," he called. "Have you your eye on anyone for a dance?"

I blushed. He saw my embarrassment and laughed.

"Don't tell me you're still a shy wee English coddie?"

I said nothing. Johnny could tease all me he liked – I wasn't wee any more, and I wasn't a coddie. I was nearly thirteen. He laughed as I turned away and followed them all into the Glen View.

The plush lobby was full of men in suits, women in their best frocks, little boys in blue velvet waistcoats, flouncy white shirts, and long grey trousers. As I came past reception there was a brown noticeboard to one side with white letters on it that said:

The Wedding Of Mr Michael O'Hanlon
and Miss Nuala McKenna
The Leinster Room

I followed my mother and my aunt and uncle as their backs disappeared into the crowd and down a carpeted hallway towards the banqueting suite.

I stood at the doors of the Leinster Room. Through tall windows panels of sunlight streaked the large saloon, great slants of gold falling criss-cross over the twenty or so tables with all of their glittering glasses, cutlery, napkin rings, crockery. For a moment I was dazzled.

My cousins were already getting seated, up towards the top table, and I walked across the deep emerald carpet to join them.

"Well, John Kevin," said Matt. "Were you ever at a wedding before?"

"No," I said, sitting down beside him.

"Do you think you'll be married one day?" asked Anna.

"Are you proposing?" I said.

"Don't be daft, John Kevin! Sure we're cousins! How could we get married?"

Johnny arrived at our table, a pint of Harp lager in his hand.

"Johnny, you shouldn't be drinking," scolded Geraldine.

"It's only rock shandy," said Johnny. "It doesn't really count. Sure there's more alcohol in my aftershave than there is in this pint."

He came and sat down by Matt, leaving one chair empty around the table. I wondered if anyone might be joining us. I turned round. A tall girl, with glossy shoulder-length black hair, large sparkling blue eyes, and a long turquoise evening gown came up and stood by Johnny. He got to his feet and made a show of introducing her.

"This is Deirdre. Deirdre, these are my sisters Geraldine, Mary, Evelyn, and Anna, and this is my brother Matt. And this here is my first cousin, John Kevin. He's from London, England. A shy wee coddie, isn't that right, John Kevin?"

"Pleased to meet you," I mumbled, standing up and offering my hand.

"At least John Kevin has manners," said Deirdre.

I blushed and we all sat down. There was a commotion behind me and I turned round. Nuala and Michael were entering the banqueting suite, Nuala in her wedding dress, Michael in his suit, smiling and nodding to people as they walked down the length of the room.

Johnny stood up and started applauding, and then everyone else was on their feet applauding too. Nuala and Michael made their way to the top table. Their parents and relatives followed them and then the rest of the guests started coming in, all in a hubbub of chat and joking and laughter, and started to find their seats. Almost at once waiters and waitresses appeared, smart in their black and whites, at our tables before we'd even noticed them.

"Would you like something to drink?"

A pretty young blonde waitress smiled at Johnny.

"Could you bring us a few bottles of red lemonade?" said Deirdre, with a smile that looked as painted on as her lipstick.

"No problem," said the waitress, and smiled back at Deirdre.

"A friend of yours?" she asked Johnny.

"No comment," he said, grinning.

The Glen View staff all disappeared through swing doors at the side of the Leinster Room, and everyone settled back to talk.

"Johnny tells me you're a great one for the books," said Deirdre.

"Did he?" I said. Johnny winked at me, but as she turned in his direction I frowned at him. The last thing I wanted was his girlfriend thinking I was some kind of bookworm. He just kept smiling and gave me another wink.

"Now – there's your lemonade."

The waitress was back, two big bottles of pop hanging by their necks in each fist. She placed them on the table and then took a small notepad out of her blouse pocket.

"What would you all like for your dinner?" she asked. "There's salmon, chicken, or beef."

I chose salmon. Everyone else asked for the beef. The waitress disappeared again, and there was an awkward silence as I tried to think of something to say to Deirdre.

"So how do you know Johnny?" I mumbled.

"I met him at a dance," she said. "He bought me a drink, we got chatting, and when the dance was over he gave me a lift home."

"And where's home?"

"Scotsville. Do you know it?"

"I know of it," I said.

"You make it sound like a thieves' kitchen, John Kevin. It's not exactly the Wild West, you know."

Now it was her turn to embarrass me.

"Ach, leave him alone," said Matt. "Sure John Kevin thinks Monaghan is full of rednecks. You wouldn't see the likes of us where he's from."

"Salmon for you, sir, beef for the rest of you."

The waitress was back, plates in her hands, more on her forearms. She started dealing them out, then dashed off to load up again. Another waitress appeared and starting placing little silver dishes of vegetables – new potatoes, peas, runner beans, carrots – in the middle of the table. The first waitress came back with more plates of beef and that was all the food laid out. As the waiters and waitresses were disappearing through the doors into the kitchen

Nuala's father stood up.

"Fr O'Shea will now say grace," he said, and sat down again.

We blessed ourselves and bowed our heads as the priest said the short prayer, and then we started. I was glad that the food gave me a chance to just get on with eating. I didn't fancy any more talking.

The rest of them turned their attention away from me. They started gossiping, Johnny saying that there were of rumours about Nuala, Geraldine telling him to not be giving out scandal, Matt joining in saying that the real scandal was how two families could make such a show of friendship when they hated each other's guts. A lot of it went over my head, but I was kind of glad of that. As long as the spotlight wasn't on me I was happy.

Desserts were served and soon the dinner was over. Nuala's father stood up again. He was a broad man, tough-looking, and his nose looked like it had been battered and broken. He hit his teaspoon off his glass and gradually the room fell silent.

"Fr O'Shea, ladies and gentlemen, I'd like to thank you all for coming here today to celebrate the wedding of Nuala and Michael. I'd like also to welcome Nuala's mother and father, Mr and Mrs O'Hanlon, all belonging to them, all here from the McKenna family, friends, acquaintances, gatecrashers, and hangers-on."

He got a few laughs, and when they died down he carried on.

"I'd also like to say a few words about Nuala. Every child is precious to their father but an only child is perhaps even more precious. I remember bringing my wife Marion home from the hospital, a tiny wee bundle in her arms. Nuala was always a happy girl. To see her there today at the altar – well, what can I say? My little girl is all grown up now. I wish her and Michael all the happiness she's known and more. Fr O'Shea, ladies and gentlemen – to Nuala and Michael."

He raised his glass and everyone in the room raised theirs with him.

Michael's father got up and called upon Shane, Michael's brother, to say a few words.

"Fr O'Shea, Ladies and Gentlemen," – and here he turned to Nuala and Michael – "Mr and Mrs O'Hanlon" – this drew warm applause – "it falls to me to welcome a new chapter in the history of our two families. I don't feel today that I'm losing a brother so much as gaining a bit more room in the house. My brother is a terrible one for taking up space, and I'm pleased that Nuala and Michael's new house is built and ready for the happy couple to move into. I was starting to think he'd never go.

"But seriously – I should say a few words by way of tribute to Michael. And don't worry – I will. But I think first, as his younger brother I would be failing in my duties if I didn't let Nuala know what she was letting herself in for. After all, there may be another Happy Event before you know it and by then it will be too late."

I'd been watching Michael's face. He suddenly turned bright red. I knew that Best Man's speeches were supposed to embarrass the groom but this was different. Something Shane said had put his brother in a rage.

Michael got up, his face crimson. He suddenly let fly with a right and thumped Shane on the nose. Blood started pouring down Shane's face. He put up his hand to check himself and looked down at the blood all over his fingers. It was like a red rag to a bull. He launched himself at Michael and grabbed him by the lapels. Shane head-butted his brother with a crack you could hear at the back of the hall. Nuala leaned over and grabbed Shane by the hair. She yanked him back quickly and hopped his noggin off the table.

This was too much for the boys' mother. Mrs O'Hanlon slapped Nuala round the face, only to be slapped in turn by Mrs McKenna. Fr O'Shea knew the game was up. He slid under the table as fast as he could while mayhem broke out around him.

I'd seen nothing like it. The fighting spread like a fever. First the table next to us started on the table next to them, then more tables joined in, punching and slapping, grappling and hair pulling, shouts and cries starting to echo around the hall.

I started to get afraid. A chair flew over my head and went sailing through the air. It crashed through one of the tall windows and then big men in black suits flooded into the Leinster Room. There was broken glass and crockery on the floor, people rolling around in it all, patches of blood on the emerald carpet.

Johnny and Matt were on their feet in front of me, slugging it out with two men, while the rest of us looked on, the girls all shouting and screaming. I ducked under the table as quickly as I could. But I as I squinted up I could just about see it all – the fighting in full flow, the big men in suits – bouncers by the looks of them – trying to restrain the scrappers and drag them apart, a kind of rumble rolling through the hall.

Suddenly a shout went up.

"You McKennas are nothing but a bunch of goatfeckers!"

As a battle cry it did the trick. For the fighting now grew more intense, the anger savage, a brutality about it all that shook me.

At that point the first of the Gardai began piling into the room. They had their truncheons out and were cracking heads as soon as they saw the carnage in front of them. One of them blew his whistle but it made no difference – the wedding guests all fought on.

But then came the battle cry again, louder, above the tumultuous din in the room.

"Goatfeckers!"

Then more shrill police whistles sliced through the air, and reinforcements from the Gardai piled in. Slowly, inch by inch, table by table, they worked their way forwards, nabbing the worst of the brawlers, getting them in arm locks, frogmarching them out, away from the carnage.

The police looked like they were getting on top of the situation. But then I saw a huge man in the middle of the room squaring up to three Guards. His wife was behind him, urging him on. He stood legs apart, fists raised, red in the face, snarling at them. A Guard came in from the side and swung his truncheon at his head. But the man saw it coming and ducked. The truncheon followed through and hit the wife smack in the mouth. Her lip split apart and blood started to run down her chin and drip onto the carpet.

This was too much. Now the brawlers turned on the Guards, and those who had been enemies a moment before were suddenly allies against the head-crackers and the hard cases in blue. What had started off as a scrap was turning into a riot. The police were caught – even the women were on their backs now, and their truncheons, whistles, and uniforms were no longer any use. They'd lost their most important weapon of all – whatever authority they'd walked in with was gone.

I looked up to the top table. Nuala was standing there, watching it all, two great tears rolling down her face. And then the table I was under went over and I felt a sharp crack to the back of my head.

I saw a whirl of stars at the back of my eyes and then I was out.

Matt sent me over the clipping from the *Northern Standard*. The Commissioner himself was called to the Glen View to take command. He had to call up reinforcements from neighbouring counties to quell the disturbance. After a pitched battle lasting several hours – I'm quoting from the report – order was restored.

Eighty-five people were arrested, an investigation held into the officer who had struck the woman – he was exonerated – and damage to the Glen View was put at £700.

Along with the clipping was a note from Matt. Nuala lost her baby. She and Michael had separated. But Gusty had got what he'd wanted. No one was ever going to forget that day.

It had been the wedding of the year.

The Carnival

The Carnival's on. What about these boys and me taking a drive out there and having some fun?"

It was Saturday afternoon. Johnny was back from Town, his MG parked next to Uncle Tommy's Beetle in the back yard, a restlessness about him. He seemed too big now for the bungalow, as if he filled up the place with wildness, like wind blowing through a chapel.

"Och, these boys are too young to be going to dances," said my mother. "Sure they're only fourteen, Johnny."

"What odds," he said. "They'll be off and away soon enough. They might as well see what the world has in store for them."

I wasn't too keen myself. But then Matt said, "Come on, Auntie Mary. Sure what's the worst that can happen? We'll look after this coddie, won't we, Johnny?"

My mother started to soften.

"All right," she said. "But no drink, no trouble, and no scandal."

"I'll be driving," said Johnny. "So that's the drink out. And I won't be looking for trouble, so there's no fear of that. As for scandal – well, you can't get up to much scandal at a dance. Not that it'll stop me trying."

He grinned and then told Matt and me to make sure we sorted out something smart to wear, that he would be back at eight for us, that he was off to see the Bank Manager.

And then he was away before anyone could even say goodbye.

"Now make sure you behave yourself tonight. I don't want to hear any tales when you get back."

My mother and I were in our room. I was getting ready, wishing Johnny would rap on the door and yell, "Come on!" Anything to get away from the lecture I knew was coming.

"Some of the lassies these days. Sure if they sneezed half of what they're wearing would fly off them."

I pulled on a green sleeveless v-neck jumper and looked at myself in the wardrobe mirror. It didn't look too bad with the salmon pink button-down shirt I was wearing. But I wasn't too sure about my trousers – black pinstripes, part of a two-piece suit my mother had bought me in Clery's in Dublin on the way up.

"You be a good boy and don't disgrace yourself."

"John Kevin! He's back! Come on, it's time to go."

I mumbled a quick goodbye to my mother, opened the door, and felt my belly turn over.

"I'm just back from Billy Brogan's kitchen," said Johnny.

The evening was still light, hardly a cloud in the sky, Matt and me stuffed in the back of the MG.

"Won me another fifty quid. So guess who's paying in and buying you a few drinks, lads?"

"You're some bucko," said Matt.

"It's all down to knowing when to hold 'em, and knowing when to fold 'em. Let's see if we can find Kenny Rogers on the dial."

Johnny turned on the car radio and started running up and down the stations looking for a bit of Country and Western.

"Wisht!" he said suddenly.

"Reports are coming in of a man abducted in Armagh by four men in balaclavas. Police have issued a statement from the mother of the kidnap victim appealing for his safe return."

The news item gave way to Tammy Wynette singing 'Stand By Your Man.'

"A bad business," said Johnny.

He drove on in silence, the countryside round about starting to darken as dusk fell. By the time we reached the Carnival the sky was pitch black. I couldn't make out any stars, or the moon.

It felt like a long way from home.

We rattled down a rutted track and came out into a big field. Before us in the MG's headlights was an enormous tent, like something you'd see if the circus had come to town. There were ropes at the sides, and a sliver of golden light in the middle – the entrance.

Johnny bumped forward over the field to the right of the tent and came to a stop. A whole fleet of cars stood there in the darkness. Little groups of ones and twos and a few small gangs were getting out of their cars, laughing and joking, and heading off towards the big tent.

"Well, boys," said Johnny. "Are you ready to have some fun?"

He turned off the ignition and pocketed the keys. I caught his eye in the rear view mirror, the wink as he looked back at me.

"Do you think you'll find yourself a woman tonight, John Kevin?"

I said nothing. He laughed and opened the door to get out and then we were out after him. Music and the sounds of the Carnival carried across the field on the warm night air and we all walked towards the big tent, following the noise.

As we came close I noticed a board outside: 'Big Tom And The Mainliners: For One Night Only. Adm: 25p." We got to the entrance and Johnny took out his wallet and pulled out a pound note.

"Three," he said to the man sitting at a table giving out tickets.

"These lads can't be drinking," said the man. "By rights I shouldn't even be letting them in."

"Don't worry, Jimmy," said Johnny. "I'll look after them."

"Go on then," said Jimmy, taking the pound off him. He gave Johnny three tickets and his change and I started to get a bit nervous. Then Johnny parted the flap and we were in.

At the far end of the tent, through a great crowd of dancers, I could just make out the musicians. Big Tom was belting out a frenzied song, his band behind him going like a train. There was a dance floor of bare boards about ten feet in front of us where a whole sea of people rocked and rolled as the waves of belting music hit them. The lyrics were something to do with squeezing her and pleasing her but they were going so fast I couldn't make it all out.

"Come on," said Johnny. "Let's get a drink."

We made our way over to a bar to the left of the dance floor. Men lined up along the counter, half of them facing the barmen trying to get a drink, half of them facing out, studying the talent. For beyond the dancers, sat at tables in two rows by the far wall of the great tent, were all the girls who'd come without partners to the Carnival. How the men at the bar, with their wolfish faces and their hungry eyes, could see through the crowd on the dance floor, I wasn't sure. But each group knew of the other. You could feel it in the air, like stormclouds.

"Three rock shandies," said Johnny.

He'd inserted himself into a space at the bar and we waited behind him. He paid the barman and handed Matt and me our pints.

"Keep an eye on that drink," he said. "I'm off to find me a woman."

"Find some for us!" said Matt.

We watched as Johnny's back disappeared into the crowd pushing forward to get served.

"Well, John Kevin," said Matt. "What do you think of it so far?"

I didn't think much of it if I was honest, the big tent, the field in the middle of nowhere, the atmosphere of desperation and longing. But all I said was, "Not bad, not bad at all," and took a sip of my drink.

"There's a fair crowd," said Matt.

"There is," I said. I got the impression he was as perplexed as I was.

"Big Tom," said Matt. "He's had more hit records in Ireland than The Beatles."

I'd never heard of him, or his band, The Mainliners. I liked T

Rex. The lyrics, mostly.

Johnny came back.

"Come on boys," he said. "Things are looking up."

He reached past us and grabbed his pint. We followed him through the push and shove of the crowd to the far side of the dance floor. Johnny walked up to a table where three girls were sitting on their own.

"Well, ladies," said Johnny. "This is my brother, Matthew, and this here is our cousin, John Kevin, from London."

He sat down on the chair facing them. The only chair. Matt and I weren't quite sure what to do. For a moment we stood looking at each other.

Johnny turned around.

"Get a couple of seats for yourselves, fellas. These girls were telling me they're all off to England once the summer is over. Training to be nurses."

Matt and I went off to fetch chairs and I thought about what Johnny had said. If these girls were going to train to be nurses that meant they were aged somewhere between sixteen and eighteen. I wondered what Johnny had told them about Matt and me.

We found a couple of chairs and brought them back to the table.

"I'm Bridget and this is my sister Bernadette, and this is Theresa, our cousin."

"And where are you girls going to train?" asked Johnny.

"We're all going to Whipp's Cross," said Bridget. "Me and Theresa are doing our SRNs and Bernadette's doing the SEN. Would you know Whipp's Cross?" she asked, turning to me.

"I would," I said.

Bridget, who looked like the eldest of the three, took this in. She was dark-haired, and wore a white blouse with tiny blue flowers embroidered on the butterfly collar. I guessed she was about eighteen. Bernadette was a little smaller, a little younger, about sixteen, with the same dark hair but her eyes were altogether larger. She had the same kind of white blouse as Bridget, but her blouse was trimmed with pink flowers, and she seemed a bit shy.

Their cousin Theresa wore a woolly brown cardigan over a pale green blouse and her complexion was much redder than the other two girls'.

"Perhaps you'll come and see us when we're over?" said Bernadette.

"That would be nice," I said, and took a sip of my shandy.

"I hear London is very big," she continued. "Are there any parts you'd recommend?"

"What Bernadette means, John Kevin," said Theresa, "is do you know any good pubs, and whether could you take us to a dance hall?"

I thought Theresa might be a little tipsy, but perhaps she was just enjoying herself.

"There's a few OK pubs near Whipp's Cross," I said, trying to sound like a man of the world, "but you have to go a bit further out to find a decent dance hall."

I'd never been in a pub or a dance hall, but I kept that to myself. Johnny grew restless in his seat.

. "Did you ever dance a girl, fellas? Here's how it's done."

Johnny stood up, looked at Bridget, cocked his finger vertically as if to say, "Come on," and off they went. I could hardly believe my eyes. But perhaps this was how things were done in Ireland. I stood up and cocked my finger at Bernadette.

What happened next happened quick.

Theresa snatched up her drink and threw it in my face. I blinked and when I opened my eyes could feel the cold liquid dripping down my cheeks. I spun on my heel and walked out. I had to get away. Away from Big Tom And The Mainliners, from the crowds, the pushing and shoving, the dancing, the humiliation. Away from the Carnival.

Under a star-scattered sky, down a moonlit road, I walked and walked before I realised I couldn't turn back. I was going to have tramp the twenty miles back to Ballydawn.

To Hell with it.

The moon passed behind some clouds and suddenly it was pitch black. The stars stood out brighter, the Milky Way as clear as an old plough in a rainy field, but cast little light on the road ahead.

The inky night was upon me and all I could do was put one uncertain foot in front of another. As I slowly grew accustomed to the dark I could make out the shape of hedges either side of me, their outlines changing as rapidly as black smoke, tapering now into the solid blackness, now billowing in my imagination like dark clouds of gas up to the sky, now running ahead straight and purposeful as I imagined them doing in daylight.

Images from the Carnival played in mind. There was Johnny, his back disappearing through the crowd to the bar, Johnny sitting down with Bridget, Bernadette, and Theresa, Johnny asking Bridget to dance, Theresa letting me have it with her drink. By now my temper was cooling and I was becoming miserable instead of mad. The night was still fairly warm but I felt little comfort trudging the road, a stranger everywhere I set my foot.

Then up ahead – miracle of miracles! – I could make out the lights of a cottage. I'd started letting my imagination get away on me, thinking the world had ended and only the darkness remained, that the sun would never rise again, that I was the only person left on Earth.

So I was glad to see that light.

But not so glad when it went out.

For now the darkness was back, somehow worse than ever.

Just then I heard the sound of an engine behind me, and moved quickly to the side of the road. A car sped past, lights dipped, a driver and their passenger gone as quickly as they'd appeared.

They didn't even see me.

I tried to work out how long it would take me to get back to Ballydawn. If Ballydawn was a mile from my aunt and uncle's house, say up to where the Protestant church marked the end of the old village, and it took ten minutes to walk there, how long would it take to walk twenty miles? Or supposing it took fifteen minutes? Or twenty? I worked out times for all of the multiples. I soon began to wish I'd never started.

When would I get there?

It must be past midnight now.
Or was it later?
I felt totally disorientated
Please God I'd make it before morning.

After long hours of walking at last I neared St Patrick's. The sun was rising as I walked past Jonjo's shop, the red garage doors next to him, the Handley brothers' cottage, and came to the bridge. I started to cross the river and took one last look at the village behind me. The river started to catch the early morning glints of sunlight falling on the ripples flowing away under the bridge and I turned and walked on. Soon I was at Maggie's Bar and passing the creamery.

I passed the last few bungalows before Auntie Lizzie and Uncle Tommy's and opened the gate. The gravel on the drive by the side of the house crunched under my feet and as I came round the back of the house I thought I could hear the radio. I lifted the latch on the back door and walked in.

There was my mother in the kitchen.

"John! Where have you been? We were all worried sick about you!"

"I walked back from the Carnival," I said. "I asked a girl to dance but her friend threw her drink in my face."

"Ach, we heard about that," said my mother.

Auntie Lizzie, Johnny, and Matt came into the kitchen.

"Come in to we see you," said my aunt. "By God, you're the quare man, John Kevin."

I said nothing but followed them all through to the front room.

"Sit down, sit down," said my mother.

I sat at the dinner table and the rest gathered round me.

"You won't have heard the news," said my mother.

"What news?" I asked.

"The lad who was abducted in Armagh. He was shot dead in a graveyard out on the Castleside road last night. Johnny and Matt got back here just after midnight. When I saw them without you I was worried sick."

"What route did you take?" asked Matt.

"I don't know," I said. "It was too dark to see where I was going. I just kind of followed my nose."

They all fell silent.

"I'm very tired," I said. "I've been walking all night. Do you mind if I go to bed?"

There wasn't much they could say.

I made my way to our room, the deep comfort of bed.

As my head touched the pillow I thought of Bernadette. I imagined asking her to dance properly this time. She accepts and soon we are dancing. I hold her close, and she murmurs in my ear.

"You're the quare man, John Kevin."

I tell her that I am, that yes, I am the quare man, and we glide across the floor.

PART III:
THE KING FROM OVER
THE WATER

The King From Over the Water

Any news?"

My mother was sitting at the table, reading a letter from my father. Sunshine streamed in through the window, and outside summer blazed with all the heat and light of a land somewhere far, far away.

"He says he'll be over next week."

She placed the letter back in its envelope and put it into her handbag. My father was supposed to be coming to Ballydawn. But there'd been a delay, and he said that he'd follow us over when he'd sorted out the "bit of business" he had to attend to.

I didn't think too much about it at first, but now I had a feeling that something was going on they weren't telling me about.

"Where's my dinner? I want it and I want it now!"

Matt pushed open the back door, the light dazzling behind him, and marched in. He was 14 that summer, working in the sawmill making boxes. My parents wanted me to "study hard at the books", so I didn't even have a paper round, or a Saturday job in the local supermarket, or any other kind of work, although my mother would sometimes get cranky about my idleness. "Books won't feed you," she'd say. My father would tell her to go easy on me, that I'd never make a doctor or a lawyer or a teacher if I didn't study.

I didn't really know what I wanted to be. All I knew is that I wanted to please them, to continue to do well at school, and have that better life they said they wanted for me.

My mother looked a little tight-faced, but I put it down to Mattie's directness.

"Your dinner's coming," she said. "Sit down there. You had to wait to be born, you'll wait for your dinner."

"Where's Mammy?" asked Matt, settling himself in the chair my mother had risen from. "Where's the rest of them?"

"Auntie Ellie has been taken bad. They've all gone up to the hospital to see her."

My mother took a few chops out of the fridge and put them on a plate. She placed the frying pan on the stove and lit the gas and soon had the chops frying.

"Taken bad?" said Matt. "How, bad?"

"They don't know," said my mother. "She fainted feeding the hens, so Seamus got her in the car and flew on up to the hospital."

"Jesus," said Matt. "Sure Auntie Ellie never had a day's illness in her life."

"It comes to us all," said my mother. "It comes to us all."

There were some left over spuds in the fridge, and now she cut these up and cooked them alongside the chops. She took out a packet of peas and started to boil up water in a pan.

"Any word from Uncle Mick?" asked Matt.

"He'll be over soon," said my mother. The same tight expression came back into her face, and I wondered again if she was trying to hide something from me, something that was going on between her and my father she didn't want me to know about. But soon my thoughts turned to food, to the chops and fried potatoes and peas, to Daddies sauce, and if there might be ice cream for afters.

"Ellie's in a bad way."

It was my uncle's turn through the back door, my aunt and my other cousins, Geraldine, Mary, Evelyn, and Anna all behind him. Johnny was away doing his national service, stationed in a barracks up in Donegal. He sent home photos of himself in uniform, looking like Elvis in Germany, parading across the square, in fatigues up in the hills, at a dance, grinning and toasting the camera, a pint of Harp lager in his hand. The house was that bit quieter without him.

"What's wrong with her, Tommy?"

"They don't know. But she's still unconscious. They said she might have something wrong with her heart."

My aunt looked red-eyed. I'd never seen Lizzie upset. She was usually so capable, baking, cooking, washing, always on the go, her six children like a small platoon she drilled every day of their lives. Up, make beds, saw sticks, run messages – Lizzie never stopped. And now it looked as if she'd been crying.

"She's my youngest sister, Mary," she said to my mother. My mother gathered up the plates, and then Lizzie cracked and was sobbing, and my mother came over to comfort her.

"She's in the best place she could be, Lizzie," she said. "I'm sure they're doing wonders for her."

Lizzie dried her eyes and stood back from my mother's embrace.

"Ellie's not coming out of that place," she said. Her tone was cold, her face sober. "I know she's not."

Mattie and I were in the front garden, sitting on the bench. The sun was still in the sky, but the heat had gone out of the day now and the cool of evening was coming in. Inside the house dinner was on the go for the rest of them and the news would soon be on.

"Do you think she'll be OK?" I said.

"I wouldn't know," said Matt.

"Your mother is taking it hard."

Matt fell silent.

"Come on," he said eventually. "Let's go in. It's getting colder."

"There's another letter from him."

We were lazing on a tartan blanket down by the stream at the end of my uncle's large back garden. The day was warm and sunny, and the midges from the stream hung in the heat. I felt somehow as if I was suspended between one world and the next, as if everything was up in the air.

My mother showed me the envelope, my father's large, old-fashioned handwriting sloping across the front of it.

"What does he say?" I asked.

She held out the letter and adjusted her glasses.

"He says he's sorry about Auntie Ellen, that he'll be over for the funeral, and to tell you to be a good boy."

"Does he say what's holding him up?" I asked.

"Divil the word. Sure you know your father. Everything on the long finger. They have a different sense of time down in Kerry. You'd think the world turned slower there."

I looked at her, sat up on the blanket, and saw again that tight expression in her face. But I couldn't fathom her, whether she was upset about Auntie Ellen, or him not being there, or something else.

I turned back to my book. Mr Tierney, my English teacher, had given me Daniel Corkery's *Hidden Ireland* to read before we broke up for the holidays, all about the Gaelic poets, and Bonnie Prince Charlie, 'The King From Over the Water', the one they all prophesied would come and save Ireland from the Saxon yoke. As I lay down by the stream at the end of the back garden I thought about those poets, and what waiting for a king who never came must have done to them.

I missed my father then and wished that he was with us, that he would come over as fast as the sea could carry him.

And then I thought of Auntie Ellen, the wake and the funeral that lay ahead, and I wondered how it would go.

"Hail Mary, full of grace, the Lord is with thee. Blessed art thou amongst women, and blessed is the fruit of thy womb, Jesus."

"Holy Mary, Mother of God, pray for us sinners, now and at the hour of our death. Amen."

My uncle was giving out the Rosary. He rattled off the Hail Marys as fast as an auctioneer selling cattle. Everyone responded to their half of the Rosary at the same breakneck pace, so that the room fairly buzzed with prayers.

I sneaked a glance through my fingers. Uncle Seamus and his

three big strapping sons, Enda, Eamon, and Declan, knelt by the open coffin in the living room, all in their best suits, Auntie Ellen laid out before them, a Rosary clasped in her cold, dead hands. The Sacred Heart looked down on them all, and as the Rosary rattled on I thought of their mother, and what her death would mean for them, four men living in a farmhouse with no wife or mother.

"Sorry for your trouble."

The mourners came out of the church and were greeted by Uncle Seamus and his sons. They all said the same thing – "Sorry for your trouble" – and then went round to the back of the church to the grave Uncle Seamus had dug.

We paid our condolences, and walked off, crunching the gravel as we went.

"No word from Mick?" said my uncle.

"No," said my mother. "No word from Mick."

Corkery's book had me entranced. The bit I liked best was about the Court of Poetry, where O'Tuama summoned poets to his shebeen out in the wilds of the West somewhere, mocking the ways of the Saxon, who were always issuing warrants and summonses to the poor Gaels. They would all meet up, and recite their verse, and send each other up, and drink. And all the while the Saxon would be out looking for them. But they'd never catch them.

The light through the window over the kitchen table suddenly darkened, and I was aware of a shadow crossing the sun. Then the back door opened and there stood my father.

"Well, John Boy," he said. "How are you doing?"

He was wearing his dark double-breasted suit, as broad as ever, a white towelling shirt open at the neck, a large black holdall in his hand. Everyone else was out, paying their respects at Auntie Ellen's grave.

He came in, smiling his horsey smile, and threw the holdall in under the table.

"It's nearly fifteen years since I was in Maggie's Bar," he said.

"Do you think they'll know me? Come on – let's get a drink."

I put down my book and followed him up the road to Maggie's. I'd never been in before. I usually got stood outside with Matt, red lemonades and a packet of Tayto to keep us quiet. But it looked as if my father meant business. He strode the few hundred yards down to the pub as if he owned the country, and I had to walk fast to keep up with him.

We came into the bar to find it deserted. It was the middle of the afternoon, and there was no one behind the counter, just the sound of the clock's loud tick echoing off the walls. My father smiled at me.

"Hello!" he shouted. "You've two thirsty customers here needing a drink! Any chance of some service?"

We heard footsteps from above as Maggie came down to see who was making all the fuss.

"Hello, Maggie," said my father. "Would you know me at all? It's fifteen years since I was here."

"Ach, Mick! How are you doing?"

"The best, Maggie, the best. I see you haven't changed a bit."

"And I can see you're still a charmer! What'll you have? A pint of Guinness is it, Mick?"

"Make it two, Maggie. One for the maneen as well."

"Ach, Mick, I can't be giving the boy drink."

"No one will know," smiled my father. "There's only us three here, and not a Guard in sight. I won't tell if you won't. And anyway, he might only be young, Maggie, but sure the boy's a man now."

I blushed at this, but Maggie smiled, and poured another. My father handed over the change, and we sat in by the door, the shade of the bar a refuge from the heat and light outside. We supped together, the Guinness dark and creamy and bitter, not saying much, and slowly the afternoon passed. He told me he meant to come over earlier, but that he'd been made redundant from his job on the railways, but had a new job, working for the council on the gardens, that it was great to see me.

The two of us sat there, drinking to each other in the shade of the bar as the long afternoon idled by, with Maggie's all to ourselves, with time enough for another, the rest of our lives before us like a prospect of the vast Atlantic Ocean.

He had come at last, my King From Over the Water.

THE BALLYDOWN CHRONICLES

The Spot in His Eye

H e turned the corner of the damp street and put a cold hand into the inside pocket of his jacket. The little notebook was still there, and he felt a quick, thrilling surge. The news had said there would be an eclipse later that evening but for now all of his excitement was focused on the address he'd written out so many times, the man he was about to meet in person. He hurried along to No 22, mounted the steps, rang the bell, and waited.

Mr Laverty opened the door.

"Come in, come in," he said. "Great to meet you at last. They're not all here yet, so come in and get warm. Do you take a whiskey, or do they make you keep your Confirmation vow in England?"

He followed Mr Laverty down the little hallway, past the font of holy water on the wall and the umbrella stand, and into the large living room that looked out onto the darkened street. A grandfather clock stood in one corner of the room, and a chintz sofa with matching armchairs nestled before the gas fire, where a fat ginger tomcat lay stretched out on a Persian rug, dreaming of mice and sparrows and the Siamese next door. Above the mantel the sorrowful face of the Sacred Heart looked down on the room, the little red lamp glowing, matching the rows of orange and blue flames flickering steadily in the grill of the gas fire. Mr Laverty went over to a drinks cabinet and picked up a bottle of Jameson's.

"Just a small one, please, Mr Laverty," he said. This was how Mr Laverty had signed off in the letters he'd sent to him in England,

and he rather liked the formal tone he used – it made him feel very grown up, as if he was corresponding with a bank manager.

Mr Laverty poured a measure into a tumbler and a larger one for himself and brought the two glasses over to where he stood warming the backs of his legs at the fire.

"Here you are," said Mr Laverty, handing him the tumbler of whiskey. "The Drumlins Writers' Circle has been in need of fresh blood for some time. That must make us all sound like a terrible bunch of old codgers. But though our great project has been many years in the making, we know it will take younger hands to see it through to completion. And ever since you answered our advertisement in the *Northern Standard*, we've all been dying to meet you."

The doorbell rang again and Mr Laverty placed his tumbler on the mantelpiece.

"Excuse me," he said, and went back out into the hallway. He heard the door opening, Mr Laverty welcoming two more members of the Drumlins Writers' Circle.

"Miss O'Shea! And Mr Corrigan! Goodness – have you both come together? Come in, come in! Our special guest for the evening is here, so come and warm yourselves and say hello."

A middle-aged woman in a tweed suit and brown shoes came trailing the cold night air behind her followed by a tall, narrow-faced man with broken veins and pale skin in a sports jacket and black slacks. Mr Laverty poured them both whiskeys and they gathered round the fire.

"We're just waiting on Mr Deery," said Mr Laverty. He had heard all about Mr Deery. He'd written over to Mr Laverty after he'd seen the advert. His cousins sent the *Northern Standard* to him every week, and he looked forward to the brown paper parcel tied up with string, the Irish stamps at once homely and foreign. Mr Laverty had told him that although the Writers' Circle very much admired Mr Deery's work, he was, alas, a bit of a wild one. The bell rang again and Mr Laverty rushed off to open the door.

"Ah, Brendan! Good of you to come!"

He heard the door opening and the tread of heavy footsteps

coming down the hall.

"Well?" said Mr Deery, coming into the living room, Mr Laverty behind him. "Are we all here?"

He was a short man, with dark, curly hair and a round, red face. His nose looked like it had been broken and reset by a butcher, and he wore a baggy dark blue suit and a white shirt open at the neck. Mr Deery seemed to be carrying a few extra pounds, a beer belly at least, but he couldn't quite be sure. That suit concealed more than it showed, and Mr Deery was all energy and bustle, striding into the room and nodding to the others, so that your eye was taken by his manner rather than his stature. A bit of a handful, he thought.

"We're all here now," said Mr Laverty. "Will you take a whiskey, Brendan?"

"I will," he answered. He eyed up the young man stood in front of fire while he waited for Mr Laverty to pour him a large one.

"So you're the boyo over from England?" he said. "The one who's been sending all the letters?"

"That's right," he said. He felt a bit awkward, standing there in front of the mantelpiece, tumbler in hand, as Mr Deery looked him up and down. "My mother was from Ballydawn. She took me over every summer for my holidays."

"And where is she now?"

"Buried up in Ballyshannon."

Mr Deery looked a little shocked, but what other way was there to put it?

"And what about your father?" asked Mr Laverty.

"He only came the once," he said, "the summer before he died."

He was blushing now, from the heat of the fire, or the whiskey, or it might have been Mr Deery's questions.

"Well, I'm sure you will have much to contribute to our great project," said Mr Laverty slowly. Having an orphan in their midst seemed to change the tenor of the evening. He started to feel awkward, as if he'd spoilt the party.

Mr Laverty handed Mr Deery a tumbler, and raised his glass.

"Slainte!" he said.

"Slainte!" they all responded, lifting their own glasses and smiling wanly at him, all except Mr Deery, who scowled as he swallowed his medicine in one gulp.

"Now why don't we sit down," said Mr Laverty, "and bring you up to date on proceedings."

The ginger tom twitched on the Persian rug, and let out a long low sigh, but no one paid it much attention. Miss O'Shea, Mr Corrigan, and Mr Laverty sat on the chintz sofa in front of the fire; himself and Mr Deery sat on the armchairs. The Drumlins Writers' Circle. His notions of becoming an author had come one step closer to fulfilment.

"The Drumlins Writers' Circle," said Mr Laverty, "has been in existence this past seven years. We've seen a few changes of personnel, but basically the Circle remains unbroken. We started out reading our stories and poems to each other, but then, one evening Brendan came up with an idea that has started a revolution."

For the first time that evening Mr Deery smiled.

"Really, Jim, it was only a bit of a Rising."

"Have it your way, Brendan, have it your way."

"If you could get to the point, Mr Laverty?" said Miss O'Shea. "Only my sister is poorly at the moment and I said I'd be back at ten o'clock to look in on her."

"Yes, yes, of course, Miss O'Shea," said Mr Laverty. "Well, after three years of us all sharing our work with each other Brendan here introduced an idea so novel, so beguiling, so captivating that all of our efforts ever since have been geared to the one end."

Mr Laverty paused, and beamed at him. He didn't quite beam back, but he let a shy smile play upon his lips.

"The Ballydawn Chronicles!" announced Mr Laverty, a cry of triumph in his voice.

"Yeah," said Mr Deery, who suddenly began speaking very fast, as if he was anxious Mr Laverty might interrupt him. "We started writing stories about an imaginary Irish village, Ballydawn we've called it, like the village out the road, the kind of place where everyone knows everyone, and the world is a very distant place. The quintessential Irish village, in other words. We have common characters, common themes, common settings —"

"But uncommon results!" broke in Mr Corrigan.

"That's right," said Miss O'Shea. "And we were just on the verge of paying Frank Maguire the printer to have a selection of our Ballydawn stories published when Mr Muldoon scarpered with the funds. I always thought he was a rogue."

"Was he never caught?" he asked.

"He wasn't," said Mr Corrigan. "But we did get a postcard from him. From America. The cheek of him!"

"Well, we'll just have to put that behind us," said Mr Laverty. "These things happen. At least we still have our grand project. In a changing Ireland, we aim to map the past and recall all our yesterdays."

"Yes," said Miss O'Shea, looking severer than ever, "before Vatican II, and RTE, and decimalisation ruined the country!"

He noted that she said nothing about the North, but let it pass. It wasn't his place to raise the issue, and anyway it seemed out of place in front of the cosy fire, the sleeping cat, the warming whiskey.

"So?" said Mr Laverty, ignoring Miss O'Shea. "Will you join us?"

He hesitated. This wasn't quite what he had been expecting. He'd thought from the ad that the Drumlins Writers' Circle was looking for members with all sorts of different stories, not a distinct programme.

"And if you have any tales to contribute, we would of course welcome them."

He thought of the notebook in his pocket, the ideas he had sketched out, the story he'd brought along specially.

"And it's still your intention to publish your work?"

"Yeah," said Brendan. "The brother works in the Court House. He reckons a book like ours would attract tourists, lots of them. Says we could get a grant for it."

His qualms evaporated at once.

"I'm in," he said.

"Great!" said Mr Laverty. "Right. Well, who would like to begin? I think we have time for one quick story tonight."

Before he could answer he heard Mr Deery say,

"I've got something, Jim. It's not quite finished, but see what you all think."

Mr Deery was away. His story would have to wait. As he settled back to listen rain started to patter away outside, bouncing off the windows, making the living room all the more warm and comfy. The eclipse would be happening soon and he wondered if the rain would leave off so he could see it.

"Perse O'Shaughnessy," said Mr Deery, "is born with a spot in his eye. Now, this isn't that unusual in the O'Shaughnessy family. All the boys are born with the spot, and it's reckoned to be a good omen, a sign of luck. The O'Shaughnessys have done well, farming, or running a creamery, something agricultural anyway."

"You haven't written any of this?" interrupted Miss O'Shea.

"No," said Brendan. "As I said, it's work in progress."

"But this is a *writers'* circle," insisted Miss O'Shea.

"There's nothing in the rules, is there?" asked Mr Deery. "About contributions being written down?"

He looked to Mr Laverty for support.

"Well, we don't really have any rules, as such," he said. "But custom and practice is that we usually read out work we've written, Brendan."

Mr Deery started to get up.

"But I suppose we could break with precedent in this case."

Mr Deery sat down again. Mr Laverty's words seemed to mollify him.

"Right. Can I go on?" he said.

"Do, please," said Mr Laverty. "We're all ears."

Mr Deery eyed them all, waited for silence, then continued.

"As I said, Perse O'Shaughnessy has the spot in his eye. But unlike his forebears he's a dreamier kind of kid altogether, so that by the time he's in his teens he's taken to dabbling in verse.

"The story opens with him idling down by the bridge, looking into the river as if he's trying to fathom his future. He's waiting on the results of his Leaving Cert, mulling over how he might make a living.

"He doesn't hear young Nancy Maguire approaching.

"'What can you see?' she asks, coming alongside him on the bridge, leaning over to scan the sluggish stretch of water.

"'I can see two idlers the day is passing,' says Perse.

"'And why shouldn't we be idle on a day like this?' says Nancy. She's a spirited girl, and she doesn't think much of this stuck-up eejit on the bridge.

> "'The busy man, the lazy fool:
> Let them be your whole life's school.
> The busy man will always eat,
> The lazy fool go in bare feet.
> For he who is busy knows
> No fear of winter winds and snows.
> Being busy thus is wise:
> Who else could say otherwise?'

"Nancy isn't expecting that. But she won't be outdone.

"'I wouldn't believe all you read in books,' she says with a sneer.

"'I didn't read it in a book,' says Perse. 'I made it up myself.'

"'A poet?' she says. 'Have you ever been in love?'

"'In love?' says Perse, looking at her coolly. She's a raven-haired beauty, about 16 or 17, with dark blue eyes that seem to flash by turns with laughter and mischief.

"'No,' he says. 'I've never been in love.'

"'Then what kind of poet are you who knows nothing of love?'

"It's his turn to feel slighted.

"'I never said I was a poet,' he says. 'At most I'm just an apprentice, that's all. It's a hobby, a pastime.'

"'Aye, and that's all it'll be,' she spits at him. 'And that's all you'll ever be, a bloody amateur penning your little sermons on the busy and the lazy!'

"'I should have learned my lesson,' says Perse. 'Don't cast your pearls before swine.'

"For a moment, Nancy is speechless. Then she throws back her head and laughs, laughs so loud she raises ripples in the stream.

"'What's so funny?' asks Perse.

"'Would you listen to the two of us?' she says. 'The Jesus of

Ballydawn, and me his lowly handmaid.'

"Perse has to admit that there's something ridiculous about the scene. The Jesus of Ballydawn. God, she's right! He starts to laugh. His laughter puts a breeze in the air.

"Ach!" said Mr Corrigan. "Why are you bothering with all that blather? Can you not just get on with it?"

"I can if I'm let," said Brendan. "Can I go on?"

"Please do," said Mr Laverty. "Please do."

"Right," said Mr Deery, giving Mr Corrigan a sharp look. "Where was I? Oh, yes! On the bridge. Right – next Nancy says,

"'Have you ever been up in Hangman's Field?'

"'Where's that?' he says.

"'Come on,' says Nancy. 'I'll show you.'

"They walk quickly over the bridge together into Ballydawn, past the pump and the cluster of shops, Perse looking slightly embarrassed the while, saying nothing to no one. At last they come to the Protestant church just beyond the village.

"'In here,' says Nancy.

"'St Mary's?' says Perse.

"'Beyond St Mary's,' says Nancy. 'It'll be like Paradise on a day like this.'

"Perse follows her until they come to the end of the church grounds. A set of rusting railings rises up before him. You would half expect to see an angel with a flaming sword standing guard."

"More blather," grumbled Mr Corrigan, but this time Mr Deery chose to ignore him.

"'Here,' says Nancy, and she shows Perse a gap in the railings. She squeezes through and he follows her, getting rust on his shirt as he goes.

"'Hangman's Field,' she says. They both look out onto a broad meadow with a line of gnarled oaks at the far end. A host of daisies and dandelions ripples across the broad expanse of grass and the sun seems to turn the whole scene to gold. Perse has never imagined that the little village of Ballydawn had anything to show so fair, but now here he is, mesmerised.

"Nancy tells him how Hangman's Field got its name. The locals reckon that a hangman from the time of '98 put up a gibbet in the meadow and killed himself on it, having hanged half the men from Ballydawn already. His days were numbered and his mind gone, shattered by the cries of the men he'd executed, who haunted him in the night. And this is where they buried him, with no cross to mark the grave, and quicklime thrown in to perish him the sooner.

"'Isn't it lovely?' says Nancy.

"Perse gives a shiver, but he has to admit that indeed it is lovely.

"From that afternoon onwards Perse and Nancy start courting. Nothing too serious mind you, just long lazy afternoons up in Hangman's Field, letting the summer works its magic of heat and light and timelessness over them.

"And so they don't notice, one warm fateful day, the pair of them in a kind of sultry trance, her seven brothers advancing towards them from the line of oak trees.

"'Nancy!' roars Seamus, the eldest brother.

"Nancy looks up in panic. Surely her brothers should have been away playing at the match today? She doesn't know that the game ended early due to a pitched battle between the two sides; they've all been sent off, and now the Maguire boys' blood is up.

"Well, Perse looks distinctly nervous, as if he's done something he shouldn't have, and been caught out. Seven tall, dark, curly-headed brothers are bearing down on him like a stormcloud passing over the summer meadow. They look as angry as a herd of bulls about to charge one nervous matador.

"'Who the hell are you?' barks Seamus.

"'I'm Perse O'Shaughnessy,' says Perse, as evenly as he can.

"'Well we're the Maguire Brothers and this is what we think of you pestering our sister.'

"Nancy is bundled out of the way, despite her protests, and then the boys set about their work. Perse is hit, punched, slapped, kneed, and kicked as if he were a Gaelic football.

"'Silence now falls on the scene. Nancy rushes to the side of the bloodied, broken Perse, her poet, her love. She cradles his head in her hands. You can see it, can't you – the sunny day, the seven brothers, Nancy, the broken body of Perse, time standing still. And of course Perse is dead – the brothers have killed him.

"'You animals!' she screams. She gets up and rushes towards Seamus. She pummels her tiny fists into his broad chest and howls at him. 'Murderer! Murderer! Murderer!' Seamus's face is white. He's never seen a dead body before, much less one he's killed himself. He grips her wrists and looks into her eyes.

"'Say nothing of this, Nancy. Blood is thicker than water.'

"'Aye, and harder to wash away!'

"'Get her out of here,' he says quietly. She breaks down in sobs, and Micheal, the second eldest of the brothers, leads her away.

"'Right,' says Seamus. 'We must hide the body. We need time to think.'

"'Surely to God we must call the priest!' cries Rory, youngest of them all.

"'Can't you see it's too late for a priest?' says Seamus. 'And no cops. We could all swing for this. And how would our poor widowed mother survive that? No – we'll have to hide the body. Come on.'

"They lift what's left of Perse and head back into the woods with him. Seamus knows of a deserted cottage in a corner of the woods that's so overgrown it's practically hidden from view. They'll hide the body there. No one questions him, no one objects. They're all in it together. They all do exactly what they're told to do. They're all in a state of shock.

"Now the boys have an uncle, Sergeant Maguire, a member of an Garda Siochana. He passes by the boys' house one evening a few months later on his bicycle.

"'Any news?' says their mother.

"It's dinner time, and they're all sat around the table, saying nothing, looking grim.

"'About the O'Shaughnessy boy?' says the uncle. 'They're combing the woods tomorrow.'

"Seamus drops his fork.

"'Seamus!' says his mother. 'What's the matter with you?'

"'Nothing,' says Seamus. 'Must have got some grease on the handle of it.'

"Nancy says nothing.

"Sergeant Maguire bids them all farewell and they listen as his bicycle ticks, ticks away out into the evening.

"That night they go back to the cottage."

"Ah, now that's a bit contrived," said Mr Corrigan. "The boys having an uncle who's a Guard."

"Perhaps Mr Deery could speed up a little," said Miss O'Shea. "I don't want to keep my sister waiting."

"I'm nearly done," said Mr Deery. "Perhaps if Tweedledum and Tweedledee didn't keep on interrupting me I might get finished quicker."

"There's no need for rudeness," huffed Miss O'Shea.

"Can I go on?" said Mr Deery. "Or shall we stop there and all go home now?"

"Please, please, Brendan," said Mr Laverty, "do continue. I'm hooked now."

"Right," said Mr Deery. "To continue."

He edged forward on the sofa, and looked into the flames in the gas fire. It was almost, he thought, as if he could see the story unspool in its little white frames like some old film. As if, almost, the story was telling itself.

"The seven brothers go equipped to the cottage," said Mr Deery.

"'Come on,' says Seamus. 'We've a good bit to do yet.'

"'But Seamus!' says Micheal. 'The stink of him!'

"'Why do you think I brought the bleach?' says Seamus. 'Come on – help me lash it around.'

"'You can't put bleach on him!' This from Joe, second youngest, looking dead scared in the light from his torch.

"'It's not for him – it's for this place, you bloody fool! The Gardai's bloodhounds will be howling from here to Hell if we don't do something about this stink.'

"'Won't it make the cops suspicious though, this place reeking of bleach?' asks Gerard, the middle brother.

"'There'll be rain in the morning. I checked the forecast. OK?'

"'OK,' says Gerard. 'You reckon the hills are the safest bet for your man, then?'

"'Aye,' says Seamus. He brings out the bottles of bleach and hands them round. 'They'll never find him up there.'

"Several months go by. One day as Seamus is sawing sticks out in the yard Uncle Freddie swings in on his bike.

"'Well, Seamus,' he says. 'How's it going?'

"Seamus looks up from his sawing.

"'Well, Uncle Freddie,' he says. 'Not too bad. How's yourself?'

"'Not great,' he says. 'The back is bad. I hear you've let your form go in the Gaelic?'

"Seamus shrugs.

"'What about your man?' he asks, as nonchalantly as he can. 'Any news?'

"'It's three months since we combed the woods,' says Freddie. 'I doubt we'll find him now.'

"'What'll ye do next then?' says Seamus.

"'Who knows?' says Freddie. 'We got wind some tinkers saw what might be a body up in the hills. We start searching there tomorrow. But I think there's nothing in it. Sure he'd be rotted away by now. But you know the O'Shaughnessys. They're putting a lot of pressure on the top brass. They won't be satisfied until they know for certain, one way or the other, exactly what happened to the boy.'

"Seamus goes back to sawing his sticks. The bastard just won't lie down, he thinks. They will all have to go through the whole bloody rigmarole again."

"Is there much more of this?" said Miss O'Shea. "Only I really should be going."

"Hold your horses," said Mr Deery. "I'm nearly done. Perhaps if you hadn't spent all night interrupting me you'd be on your way by now!"

He was eager for him to continue. How was this story going to turn out? What were the boys going to do? Would Nancy tell on them? And did Uncle Freddie know more than he was letting on? Very crafty, that uncle.

"Right. This is the last part of it coming up now. If you all keep quiet I can be done by a quarter to ten."

There was silence again in the room, broken only by the sound of the rain drumming a tattoo on the window, and faintly in the distance thunder rolling in over the drumlins.

"Seamus calls a meeting of the brothers," continued Mr Deery.

"'Where to this time?' asks Michael.

"'We'll put him down the Caves,' says Seamus. 'They won't find him there.'

"But the other brothers start to get queasy.

"'Surely to God somebody should inform his parents,' says Gerard.

"'Somebody already has,' says Seamus quietly. 'I sent them a letter telling them their son was dead. Anonymous, of course.'

"There's uproar now from the brothers. If Seamus is just going to go ahead and act on his own, without consulting them – well, he can move the bloody body on his own as well. They want no more of it.

"Seamus is stubborn. OK, if that's the way they want it, that's the way it has to be.

"He goes to get his bike from the garage. He can hear a snuffling sound from inside, and when he opens the door there's Nancy, sitting on a stool, slumped over a workbench, sobbing in the gloom of the garage.

"'Now, now, Nancy,' he says, coming towards her. 'This won't do.'

"'I miss him so much, Seamus, I miss him…' She breaks down again, and buries her head in her arms on the workbench.

"Seamus strokes her hair before speaking.

"'He was a blackguard, Nancy. Surely you know that?'

"'He was not!' She shoots round at him, and even in the gloom he can see the wild fire in her eyes. 'He was a good boy, gentle, kind, better than any of ye will ever be!'

"'Well, if he was so good…' says Seamus.

"'It's not what you think at all!' she cries, rising from the stool and dashing out into the weak winter sunlight.

"Seamus admires his sister's loyalty, but he knows it's misplaced.

Nancy's bulging belly is proof of that. So off he goes to the hills, to remove what's left of poor Perse and put him down the Caves.

"A few weeks go by and Uncle Freddie is stretching himself out in front of the turf fire in Maggie's Bar.

"'Got another report of a body being sighted,' he says. 'Supposed to be in a terrible state. Practically a skeleton.'

"Seamus is sat opposite him, drinking a mineral.

"'Oh? And where was that?' he asks, as coolly as he can.

"'Some tourists came across it in the Caves,' says Freddie. 'Potholing. Said it was deep down but not deep enough to hide the smell. Drew them like bloodhounds apparently. A pathologist from Dublin has been sent for. He should be here in the morning.'

"'And where's the body now?' asks Seamus.

"'Still there,' says Freddie. 'One of the potholer chaps, English fellow, is going down with our boys tomorrow.'

"'So not a false alarm like the tinkers then?' says Seamus.

"'Oh, no. Not at all. They took a photograph, you see.'

"Seamus tries not to react.

"'Any good?' he manages to say.

"'Near turned my hair white, boy,' says Freddie. 'Dr Kilbannon says almost definitely a male though.'

"'How can he tell?' says Seamus.

"'Size of the skull,' says Freddie. 'A shame the eyes are gone though. The spot would have put the matter completely beyond doubt.'

"'Sweet Jesus!' thinks Seamus. 'The net is closing in!'

"The scene switches to the Caves. They're at their most treacherous now. Underground streams criss-cross their deeper reaches and the thaw after winter's freeze makes them doubly dangerous. You could find yourself trapped in a chamber that will rapidly fill up with stone-cold water. You'd either be lost or drowned.

"Seamus is well aware of these risks though. His father made good use of the Caves back in Twenty-two. They'd been a place of refuge, a place used by men who had fought for Ireland, then ended up fighting each other. And when all the fighting was done, and a Free State rose from the ashes of battle, Seamus's father used to take the boys to the Caves every summer, and tell them tales of his youth, of skirmishes and ambushes, advances and retreats, and sometimes show them where a traitor had met his last. Death is no stranger to those deep, dark places out in the wilds of the county."

A great fork of lightning suddenly lit up Mr Laverty's living room, the electric whiteness of the bolt vivid against the black night. Thunder crashed loudly overhead and the rain lashed the windows now like a banshee wailing for release.

"God between us and all harm!" cried Miss O'Shea. "Jesus, Mary, and Joseph, Mr Deery, would you ever get to the end of this story!"

"You'll be in no rush now," said Mr Deery. "The storm is right overhead, and you may as well wait for it to die down before you venture out."

He was right: there was nothing for it now but to hear the tale to the very end. Miss O'Shea's sister would have to be patient.

And so, as the thunder and lightning crashed and flashed around them, they settled down to listen to the end of Mr Deery's story.

"Seamus doesn't take much in the way of equipment," says Mr Deery. "Typical of the English to make an expedition out of a bit of fun. The Caves' echoing darkness holds very few mysteries for him. Perse is down here somewhere. He's got a pretty good idea of where he left him. He just hopes the chamber isn't flooded: the cold water will make recovery impossible for Seamus, but not for the determined crew the Guards will be bringing along in the morning. He presses on.

"After hours in the damp and the dark he comes at last to the deep chamber where he left Perse. But he's not there.

"Seamus begins to panic. It will be light soon, another three or four hours at the most, and there's no sign of the bones, the skull, the remains of the boy who has blackguarded his sister. He feels like they're watching him somewhere, that in some grim game of tig they're playing hide-and-seek, chuckling away at him.

"He shakes his head. Foolish notions. He's following a stream now from the chamber where he left the body all those weeks ago.

He thinks the bones may have been carried away on an eddy of the central underground river. They've either been swept away by the stream, or he's confused about where he left them, and they're in some nearby chamber of the Caves' huge substructure. Seamus starts to grow hopeful. He reckons the stream will lead him to the bones, that they'll soon be his again. He feels a kind of comradely regard for them then. You may have had your fun with me, boy, he murmurs, but I'll have you soon. And then I'll make sure you don't trouble me again.

"He continues wading through the stream, his torch casting a beam ahead of him. Then he sees a shape in the gloom. On a ledge just up ahead, in the light from his torch, are the remains of Perse O'Shaugnessy, a bundle of scattered white bones in the damp and darkness of the Caves. He's found him at last."

Another huge bolt of lightning rent the night sky, and thunder rolled across the deep darkness. The eerie, terrifying light seemed to pierce the warmth and cosiness of Mr Laverty's living room, and everyone jumped a foot, all except Mr Deery. He was grinning now, enjoying the power he had over them all, the power, it would seem, he had over the very elements. No one could take their eyes off him, illuminated as he was by the lightning bolts flashing around him.

"Seamus emerges at last into the first grey gleams of dawn," continued Mr Deery, all eyes on him. "A bag of bones is rattling over his shoulder as he walks along. He would have to be careful to keep out of sight of the Guards and their search party. But he's on the last lap now. He's off to the river, to the bridge that crosses it on the road into Ballydawn. Fat with the fall of several days' rain, the river will devour these bones and carry them out to sea. Seamus would be done with them then. He feels at last a surge of optimism about all of this. What he'd done he'd done for the sake of Nancy and his brothers. Blood is thicker than water. Luckily there is none left now to float to the surface."

Mr Deery paused and looked round triumphantly. He had them all now.

"When Nancy has her baby a month later, folks in Ballydawn

aren't surprised. The pressure she's under. The scandal she's brought on herself and her family. Her mother has taken it all with a resigned air, as a widow, perhaps, would. She has never put pressure on Nancy to reveal who the father is. Her daughter's been in a fix and Mrs Maguire has drawn closer to her the more the tongues have wagged. And so Nancy's boy comes into the world. That he has blue eyes without a hint of a spot in them is remarked on by no one. But things will never be the same again for Seamus and his brothers."

By now the storm had broken, the thunder and lightning abated, and the silence that had fallen over the drenched world come just as Mr Deery got to the end of his story. He looked around the room, and waited for a reaction.

"Well, I must be going," said Miss O'Shea primly. "Thank you as ever for your hospitality, Mr Laverty."

She rose stiffly, and Mr Laverty rose with her. Mr Corrigan stood up also.

"I should be off myself," he said. "The wife will be worried about me in this weather. See you again, Mr Laverty."

"Yes, yes," said Mr Laverty, fussing over them. "Let me show you to the door. Will you be needing umbrellas? I have some here in the hall."

He was left alone with Mr Deery, and the cat sleeping soundly by the fire.

"Well?" said Mr Deery. "What did you think? Obviously too much for those two. They couldn't wait to get out of here. But I scared the wits out them. What did you think?"

But before he could reply Mr Laverty came back into the room.

"Well, they're gone now," he said. "Will you boys have another Jameson's?"

As Mr Laverty went over to fix the drinks, he looked out of the window. The rain had cleared now, and as he looked up into the sky he saw the moon looking down, a small black cloud in front, for all the world like a huge eye with a spot in the corner of it.

"There you are, boys," said Mr Laverty handing out the drinks. He took his tumbler of whiskey and gazed out again at the night.

As he looked the moon seemed to wink at him, a long slow sly wink, and he remembered the eclipse. But then a larger cloud passed over the face of the moon, and when it appeared again it was as if the wink had never happened.

"Well," said Mr Laverty, settling down with his drink. "Wasn't it a grand story? Now, what do you think?"

He turned his attention to the two men in the room, the kindly Mr Laverty and the deadly Mr Deery. He took a sip of his whiskey, and let the fire of it warm him.

At last it was his turn to speak.

Acknowledgements

The King From Over the Water first became a possibility when Jonathan Conway, my old literary agent, encouraged me to write this book, and I'll always be grateful to him for his belief in Ballydawn. But even before Jonathan's prompting, my Monaghan cousins Johnny, Geraldine, Matthew, Mary, Evelyn, and Anna, their mother and father, my Uncle Tommy and Auntie Lizzie, and my own mother and father, were inspiring what I have dreamt up here. The Royal Literary Fund and Arts Council England both kept me going during the writing of the book. I also pay tribute to two London friends: Doris Daly, and Lorna O'Connell, who both gave me great support and encouragement along the way. Jackie Gorman read an earlier version of *The King From Over the Water* and also bolstered my belief in its worth. Gavin Clarke of the Irish Literary Society has been very helpful in ensuring this book gets a wider window on the world, and my friend David Pollard has been a long-standing supporter of the stories, and a generous patron. Without the help of Bob Carling and Maria C. McCarthy this book could not have been published. Finally, to my wife Bernadette and children Max, Myles, Sean, and Caitlin, who put up with me reading bits of this out to them – your patience and love sustains me.

Lightning Source UK Ltd.
Milton Keynes UK
UKHW010945201120
373762UK00003B/635

9 781999 375300